L'Abbé Constantin

L'Abbé Constantin

Ludovic Halévy

With an Introduction By
E. Legouve
de l'Académie Française

ÆGYPAN PRESS

L'Abbé Constantin
A publication of
ÆGYPAN PRESS

www.aegypan.com

Ludovic Halévy

Ludovic Halévy was born in Paris, January 1, 1834. His father was Leon Halévy, the celebrated author; his grandfather, Fromenthal, the eminent composer. Ludovic was destined for the civil service, and, after finishing his studies, entered successively the Department of State (1852); the Algerian Department (1858), and later on became editorial secretary of the Corps Legislatif (1860). When his patron, the Duc de Morny, died in 1865, Halévy resigned, giving up a lucrative position for the uncertain profession of a playwright: At this period he devoted himself exclusively to the theater.

He had already written plays as early as 1856, and had also tried his hand at fiction, but did not meet with very great success. Toward 1860, however, he became acquainted with Henri Meilhac, and with him formed a kind of literary union, lasting for almost twenty years, when Halévy rather abruptly abandoned the theater and became a writer of fiction.

We have seen such kinds of co-partnerships, for instance, in Beaumont and Fletcher; more recently in the beautiful French tales of Erckmann-Chatrian, and still later in the English novels of Besant and Rice.

Some say it was a fortunate event for Meilhac; others assert that Halévy reaped a great profit by the union. Be this as it may, a great number of plays — drama, comedy, farce, opera, operetta and ballet — were jointly produced, as is shown by the title-pages of two score or more of their pieces. When Ludovic Halévy was a candidate for L'Académie — he entered that glorious body in 1884 — the question was ventilated by Pailleron: "What was the author's literary relation in his union with Meilhac?" It was answered by M. Sarcey, who criticized the character and quality of the work achieved. Public opinion has a long time since brought in quite another verdict in the case.

Halévy's cooperation endowed the plays of Meilhac with a fuller ethical richness — tempered them, so to speak, and made them real, for it cannot be denied that Meilhac was inclined to extravagance.

Halévy's novels are remarkable for the elegance of literary style, tenderness of spirit and keenness of observation. He excels in ironical sketches. He has often been compared to Eugène Sue, but his touch is lighter than Sue's, and his humor less unctuous. Most of his little sketches, originally written for *La Vie Parisienne*, were collected in his *Monsieur et Madame Cardinal* (1873); and *Les Petites Cardinal*, (1880). They are not intended *virginibus puerisque*, and the author's attitude is that of a half-pitying, half-contemptuous moralist, yet the virility of his criticism has brought him immortality.

Personal recollections of the great war are to be found in *L'Invasion* (1872); and *Notes et Souvenirs*, 1871–1872 (1889). Most extraordinary, however, was the success of *L'Abbé Constantin* (1882), crowned by the Academy, which has gone through no less than one hundred and fifty editions up to 1904, and ranks as one of the greatest successes of contemporaneous literature. It is, indeed, his *chef-d'œuvre*, very delicate, earnest, and at the same time ironical, a most entrancing family story. It was then that the doors of the French Academy opened wide before Halévy. *L'Abbé Constantin* was adapted for the stage by Cremieux and Decourcelle (Le Gymnase, 1882). Further notable novels are: *Criquette, Deux Mariages, Un Grand Mariage, Un Mariage d'Amour,* all in 1883; *Princesse, Les Trois Coups de Foudre, Mon Camarade Moussard,* all in 1884; and the romances, *Karikari* (1892), and *Mariette* (1893). Since that time, I think, Halévy has not published anything of importance.

E. Legouve
de l'Académie Française

Chapter I

THE SALE OF LONGUEVAL

*W*ith a step still valiant and firm, an old priest walked along the dusty road in the full rays of a brilliant sun. For more than thirty years the Abbé Constantin had been Curé of the little village which slept there in the plain, on the banks of a slender stream called La Lizotte. The Abbé Constantin was walking by the wall which surrounded the park of the castle of Longueval; at last he reached the entrance-gate, which rested high and massive on two ancient pillars of stone, embrowned and gnawed by time. The Curé stopped, and mournfully regarded two immense blue posters fixed on the pillars.

The posters announced that on Wednesday, May 18, 1881, at one o'clock P.M., would take place, before the Civil Tribunal of Souvigny, the sale of the domain of Longueval, divided into four lots:

1. The castle of Longueval, its dependencies, fine pieces of water, extensive offices, park of 150 hectares in extent, completely surrounded by a wall, and traversed by the little river Lizotte. Valued at 600,000 francs.
2. The farm of Blanche-Couronne, 300 hectares, valued at 500,000 francs.
3. The farm of La Rozeraie, 250 hectares, valued at 400,000 francs.
4. The woods and forests of La Mionne, containing 450 hectares, valued at 550,000 francs.

And these four amounts, added together at the foot of the bill, gave the respectable sum of 2,050,000 francs.

Then they were really going to dismember this magnificent domain, which, escaping all mutilation, had for more than two centuries always been transmitted intact from father to son in the family of Longueval. The placards also announced that after the temporary division into four lots, it would be possible to unite them again, and offer for sale the entire domain; but it was a very large morsel, and, to all appearance, no purchaser would present himself.

The Marquise de Longueval had died six months before; in 1873 she had lost her only son, Robert de Longueval; the three heirs were the grandchildren of the Marquise: Pierre, Hélène, and Camille. It had been found necessary to offer the domain for sale, as Hélène and Camille were minors. Pierre, a young man of three-and-twenty, had lived rather fast, was already half-ruined, and could not hope to redeem Longueval.

It was mid-day. In an hour it would have a new master, this old castle of Longueval; and this master, who would he be? What woman would take the place of the old Marquise in the chimney-corner of the grand salon, all adorned with ancient tapestry? — the old Marquise, the friend of the old priest. It was she who had restored the church; it was she who had established and furnished a complete dispensary at the vicarage under the care of Pauline, the Curé's servant; it was she who, twice a week, in her great barouche, all crowded with little children's clothes and thick woolen petticoats, came to fetch the Abbé Constantin to make with him what she called *la chasse aux pauvres.*

The old priest continued his walk, musing over all this; then he thought, too — the greatest saints have their little weaknesses — he thought, too, of the beloved habits of thirty years thus rudely interrupted. Every Thursday and every Sunday he had dined at the castle. How he had been petted, coaxed, indulged! Little Camille — she was eight years old — would come and sit on his knee and say to him:

"You know, Monsieur le Curé, it is in your church that I mean to be married, and grandmamma will send such heaps of flowers to fill, quite fill the church — more than for the month of Mary. It will be like a large garden — all white, all white, all white!"

The month of Mary! It was then the month of Mary. Formerly, at this season, the altar disappeared under the flowers brought from the conservatories of Longueval. None this year were on the altar, except a few bouquets of lily-of-the-valley and white lilac in gilded china vases. Formerly, every Sunday at high mass, and every evening during the month of Mary, Mademoiselle Hebert, the reader to Madame de Longueval, played the little harmonium given by the Marquise. Now the poor harmonium, reduced to silence, no longer accompanied the voices of the choir or the children's hymns. Mademoiselle Marbeau, the postmistress, would, with all her heart, have taken the place of Mademoiselle Hebert, but she dared not, though she was a little musical! She was afraid of being remarked as of the clerical party, and denounced by the Mayor, who was a Freethinker. That might have been injurious to her interests, and prevented her promotion.

He had nearly reached the end of the wall of the park — that park of which every corner was known to the old priest. The road now followed the banks of the Lizotte, and on the other side of the little stream stretched the fields belonging to the two farms; then, still farther off, rose the dark woods of La Mionne.

Divided! The domain was going to be divided! The heart of the poor priest was rent by this bitter thought. All that for thirty years had been inseparable, indivisible to him. It was a little his own, his very own, his estate, this great property. He felt at home on the lands of Longueval. It had happened more than once that he had stopped complacently before an immense cornfield, plucked an ear, removed the husk, and said to himself:

"Come! the grain is fine, firm, and sound. This year we shall have a good harvest!"

And with a joyous heart he would continue his way through his fields, his meadows, his pastures; in short, by every chord of his heart, by every tie of his life, by all his habits, his memories, he clung to this domain whose last hour had come.

The Abbé perceived in the distance the farm of Blanche-Couronne; its red-tiled roofs showed distinctly against the verdure of the forest. There, again, the Curé was at home. Bernard, the farmer of the Marquise, was his friend; and when the old priest was delayed in his visits to the poor and sick, when the sun was sinking below the horizon, and the Abbé began to feel a little fatigued in his limbs, and a sensation of exhaustion in his stomach, he stopped and supped with Bernard, regaled himself with a savory stew and potatoes, and emptied his pitcher of cider; then, after supper, the farmer harnessed his old black mare to his cart, and took the vicar back to Longueval. The whole distance they chatted and quarreled. The Abbé reproached the farmer with not going to mass, and the latter replied:

"The wife and the girls go for me. You know very well, Monsieur le Curé, that is how it is with us. The women have enough religion for the men. They will open the gates of paradise for us."

And he added maliciously, while giving a touch of the whip to his old black mare:

"If there is one!"

The Curé sprang from his seat.

"What! if there is one! Of a certainty there is one."

"Then you will be there, Monsieur le Curé. You say that is not certain, and I say it is. You will be there, you will be there, at the gate, on the watch for your parishioners, and still busy with their little affairs; and you will say to St. Peter — for it is St. Peter, isn't it, who keeps the keys of paradise?"

"Yes, it is St. Peter."

"Well, you will say to him, to St. Peter, if he wants to shut the door in my face under the pretense that I did not go to mass — you will say to him: 'Bah! let him in all the same. It is Bernard, one of the farmers of Madame la Marquise, an honest man. He was common councilman, and he voted for the maintenance of the sisters when they were going to be expelled from the village school.' That will touch St. Peter, who will answer: 'Well, well, you may pass, Bernard, but it is only to please Monsieur le Curé.' For you will be Monsieur le Curé up there, and Curé of Longueval, too, for paradise itself would be dull for you if you must give up being Curé of Longueval."

Curé of Longueval! Yes, all his life he had been nothing but Curé of Longueval, had never dreamed of anything else, had never wished to be anything else. Three or four times excellent livings, with one or two curates, had been offered to him, but he had always refused them. He loved his little church, his little village, his little vicarage. There he had it all to himself, saw to everything himself; calm, tranquil, he went and came, summer and winter, in sunshine or storm, in wind or rain. His frame became hardened by fatigue and exposure, but his soul remained gentle, tender, and pure.

He lived in his vicarage, which was only a larger laborer's cottage, separated from the church by the churchyard. When the Curé mounted the ladder to train his pear and peach trees, over the top of the wall he perceived the graves over which he had said the last prayer, and cast the first spadeful of earth. Then, while continuing his work, he said in his heart a little prayer for the repose of those among his dead whose fate disturbed him, and who might be still detained in purgatory. He had a tranquil and childlike faith.

But among these graves there was one which, oftener than all the others, received his visits and his prayers. It was the tomb of his old friend Dr. Reynaud, who had died in his arms in 1871, and under what circumstances! The doctor had been like Bernard; he never went to mass or to confession; but he was so good, so charitable, so compassionate to the suffering. This was the cause of the Curé's great anxiety, of his great solicitude. His friend Reynaud, where was he? Where was he? Then he called to mind the noble life of the country doctor, all made up of courage and self-denial; he recalled his death, above all his death, and said to himself:

"In paradise; he can be nowhere but in paradise. The good God may have sent him to purgatory just for form's sake — but he must have delivered him after five minutes."

All this passed through the mind of the old man, as he continued his walk toward Souvigny. He was going to the town, to the solicitor of the Marquise, to inquire the result of the sale; to learn who were to be the new masters of the castle of Longueval. The Abbé had still about a mile to walk before reaching the first houses of Souvigny, and was passing the park of Lavardens when he heard, above his head, voices calling to him:

"Monsieur le Curé, Monsieur le Curé."

At this spot adjoining the wall, a long alley of lime trees bordered the terrace, and the Abbé, raising his head, perceived Madame de Lavardens, and her son Paul.

"Where are you going, Monsieur le Curé?" asked the Countess.

"To Souvigny, to the Tribunal, to learn —"

"Stay here — Monsieur de Larnac is coming after the sale to tell me the result."

The Abbé Constantin joined them on the terrace.

Gertrude de Lannilis, Countess de Lavardens, had been very unfortunate. At eighteen she had been guilty of a folly, the only one of her life, but that one — irreparable. She had married for love, in a burst of enthusiasm and exaltation, M. de Lavardens, one of the most fascinating and brilliant men of his time. He did not love her, and only married her from necessity; he had devoured his patrimonial fortune to the very last farthing, and for two or three years had supported himself by various expedients. Mademoiselle de Lannilis knew all that, and had no illusions on these points, but she said to herself:

"I will love him so much, that he will end by loving me."

Hence all her misfortunes. Her existence might have been tolerable, if she had not loved her husband so much; but she loved him too much. She had only succeeded in wearying him by her importunities and tenderness. He returned to his former life, which had been most irregular. Fifteen years had passed thus, in a long martyrdom, supported by Madame de Lavardens with all the appearance of passive resignation. Nothing ever could distract her from, or cure her of, the love which was destroying her.

M. de Lavardens died in 1869; he left a son fourteen years of age, in whom were already visible all the defects and all the good qualities of his father. Without being seriously affected, the fortune of Madame de Lavardens was slightly compromised, slightly diminished. Madame de Lavardens sold her mansion in Paris, retired to the country, where she lived with strict economy, and devoted herself to the education of her son.

But here again grief and disappointment awaited her. Paul de Lavardens was intelligent, amiable, and affectionate, but thoroughly rebellious against any constraint, and any species of work. He drove to despair three or four tutors who vainly endeavored to force something serious into his head, went up to the military college of Saint-Cyr, failed at the examination, and began to devour in Paris, with all the haste and folly possible, 200,000 or 300,000 francs.

That done, he enlisted in the first regiment of the Chasseurs d'Afrique, had in the very beginning of his military career the good fortune to make one of an expeditionary column sent into the Sahara, distinguished himself, soon became quartermaster, and at the end of three years was about to be appointed sub-lieutenant, when he was captivated by a young person who played the *Fille de Madame Angot,* at the theater in Algiers.

Paul had finished his time, he quitted the service, and went to Paris with his charmer. . . . then it was a dancer. . . . then it was an actress. . . . then a circus-rider. He tried life in every form. He led the brilliant and miserable existence of the unoccupied.

But it was only three or four months that he passed in Paris each year. His mother made him an allowance Of 30,000 francs, and had declared to him that never, while she lived, should he have another penny before his marriage. He knew his mother, he knew he must consider her words as serious. Thus, wishing to make a good figure in Paris, and lead a merry life, he spent his 30,000 francs in three months, and then docilely returned to Lavardens, where he was "out at grass." He spent his time hunting, fishing, and riding with the officers of the artillery regiment quartered at Souvigny. The little provincial milliners and grisettes replaced, without rendering him obvious of, the little singers and actresses of Paris. By searching for them, one may still find grisettes in country towns, and Paul de Lavardens sought assiduously.

As soon as the Curé had reached Madame de Lavardens, she said: "Without waiting for Monsieur de Larnac, I can tell you the names of the purchasers of the domain of Longueval. I am quite easy on the subject, and have no doubt of the success of our plan. In order to avoid any foolish disputes, we have agreed among ourselves, that is, among our neighbors, Monsieur de Larnac, Monsieur Gallard, a great Parisian banker, and myself. Monsieur de Larnac will have La Mionne, Monsieur Gallard the castle and Blanche-Couronne, and La Rozeraie. I know you, Monsieur le Curé, you will be anxious about your poor, but comfort yourself. These Gallards are rich and will give you plenty of money."

At this moment a cloud of dust appeared on the road, from it emerged a carriage.

"Here comes Monsieur de Larnac!" cried Paul, "I know his ponies!"

All three hurriedly descended from the terrace and returned to the castle. They arrived there just as M. de Larnac's carriage drove up to the entrance.

"Well?" asked Madame de Lavardens.

"Well!" replied M. de Larnac, "we have nothing."

"What? Nothing?" cried Madame de Lavardens, very pale and agitated.

"Nothing, nothing; absolutely nothing — the one or the other of us."

And M. de Larnac springing from his carriage, related what had taken place at the sale before the Tribunal of Souvigny.

"At first," he said, "everything went upon wheels. The castle went to Monsieur Gallard for 650,000 francs. No competitor — a raise of fifty francs had been sufficient. On the other hand, there was a little battle for Blanche-Couronne. The bids rose from 500,000 francs to 520,000 francs, and again Monsieur Gallard was victorious. Another and more animated battle for La Rozeraie; at last it was knocked down to you, Madame, for 455,000 francs. . . . I got the forest of La Mionne without opposition at a rise of 100 francs. All seemed over, those present had risen, our solicitors were surrounded with persons asking the names of the purchasers."

"Monsieur Brazier, the judge entrusted with the sale, desired silence, and the bailiff of the court offered the four lots together for 2,150,000 or 2,160,000 francs, I don't remember which. A murmur passed through the assembly. 'No one will bid' was heard on all sides. But little Gibert, the solicitor, who was seated in the first row, and till then had given no sign of life, rose and said calmly, 'I have a purchaser for the four lots together at 2,200,000 francs.' This was like a thunderbolt. A tremendous clamor arose, followed by a dead silence. The hall was filled with farmers and laborers from the neighborhood. Two million francs! So much money for the land threw them into a sort of respectful stupor. However, Monsieur Gallard, bending toward Sandrier, the solicitor who had bid for him, whispered something in his ear. The struggle began between Gibert and Sandrier. The bids rose to 2,500,000 francs. Monsieur Gallard hesitated for a moment — decided — continued up to 3,000,000. Then he stopped and the whole went to Gibert. Everyone rushed on him, they surrounded — they crushed him: 'The name, the name of the purchaser?' 'It is an American,' replied Gibert, 'Mrs. Scott.'"

"Mrs. Scott!" cried Paul de Lavardens.

"You know her?" asked Madame de Lavardens.

"Do I know her? — do I — not at all. But I was at a ball at her house six weeks ago."

"At a ball at her house! and you don't know her! What sort of woman is she, then?"

"Charming, delightful, ideal, a miracle!"

"And is there a Mr. Scott?"

"Certainly, a tall, fair man. He was at his ball. They pointed him out to me. He bowed at random right and left. He was not much amused, I will answer for it. He looked at us as if he were thinking, 'Who are all these people? What are they doing at my house?' We went to see Mrs. Scott and Miss Percival, her sister. And certainly it was well worth the trouble."

"These Scotts," said Madame de Lavardens, addressing M. de Larnac, "do you know who they are?"

"Yes, Madame, I know. Mr. Scott is an American, possessing a colossal fortune, who settled himself in Paris last year. As soon as their name was mentioned, I understood that the victory had never been doubtful. Gallard was beaten beforehand. The Scotts began by buying a house in Paris for 2,000,000 francs, it is near the Parc Monceau."

"Yes, Rue Murillo," said Paul; "I tell you I went to a ball there. It was —"

"Let Monsieur de Larnac speak. You can tell us presently about the ball at Mrs. Scott's."

"Well, now, imagine my Americans established in Paris," continued M. de Larnac, "and the showers of gold begun. In the orthodox parvenu style they amuse themselves with throwing handfuls of gold out of window. Their great wealth is quite recent, they say; ten years ago Mrs. Scott begged in the streets of New York."

"Begged!"

"They say so. Then she married this Scott, the son of a New York banker, and all at once a successful lawsuit put into their hands not millions, but tens of millions. Somewhere in America they have a silver mine, but a genuine mine, a real mine — a mine with silver in it. Ah! we shall see what luxury will reign at Longueval! We shall all look like paupers beside them! It is said that they have 100,000 francs a day to spend."

"Such are our neighbors!" cried Madame de Lavardens. "An adventuress! and that is the least of it — a heretic, Monsieur l'Abbé, a Protestant!"

A heretic! a Protestant! Poor Curé; it was indeed that of which he had immediately thought on hearing the words, "An American, Mrs. Scott." The new chatelaine of Longueval would not go to mass. What did it matter to him that she had been a beggar? What did it matter to him if she possessed tens and tens of millions? She was not a Catholic. He would never again baptize children born at Longueval, and the chapel in the castle, where he had so often said mass, would be transformed into a Protestant oratory, which would echo only the frigid utterances of a Calvinistic or Lutheran pastor.

Everyone was distressed, disappointed, overwhelmed; but in the midst of the general depression Paul stood radiant.

"A charming heretic at all events," said he, "or rather two charming heretics. You should see the two sisters on horseback in the Bois, with two little grooms behind them not higher than that."

"Come, Paul, tell us all you know. Describe the ball of which you speak. How did you happen to go to a ball at these Americans?"

"By the greatest chance. My Aunt Valentine was at home that night; I looked in about ten o'clock. Well, Aunt Valentine's Wednesdays are not exactly scenes of wild enjoyment, I give you my word! I had been there about twenty minutes when I caught sight of Roger de Puymartin escaping furtively. I caught him in the hall and said:

"'We will go home together.'

"'Oh! I am not going home.'

"'Where are you going?'

"'To the ball.'

"'Where?'

"'At Mrs. Scott's. Will you come?'

"'But I have not been invited.'

"'Neither have I'

"'What! not invited?'

"'No. I am going with one of my friends.'

"'And does your friend know them?'

"'Scarcely; but enough to introduce us. Come along; you will see Mrs. Scott.'

"'Oh! I have seen her on horseback in the Bois.'

"'But she does not wear a low gown on horseback; you have not seen her shoulders, and they are shoulders which ought to be seen. There is nothing better in Paris at this moment.'

"And I went to the ball, and I saw Mrs. Scott's red hair, and I saw Mrs. Scott's white shoulders, and I hope to see them again when there are balls at Longueval."

"Paul!" said Madame de Lavardens, pointing to the Abbé.

"Oh! Monsieur l'Abbé, I beg a thousand pardons. Have I said anything? It seems to me —"

The poor old priest had heard nothing; his thoughts were elsewhere. Already he saw, in the village streets, the Protestant pastor from the castle stopping before each house, and slipping under the doors little evangelical pamphlets.

Continuing his account, Paul launched into an enthusiastic description of the mansion, which was a marvel —

"Of bad taste and ostentation," interrupted Madame de Lavardens.

"Not at all, mother, not at all; nothing startling, nothing loud. It is admirably furnished, everything done with elegance and originality. An incomparable conservatory, flooded with electric light; the buffet was placed in the conservatory under a vine laden with grapes, which one could gather by handfuls, and in the month of April! The accessories of the cotillon cost, it appears, more than 400,000 francs. Ornaments, *bon-bonnieres*, delicious trifles, and we were begged to accept them. For my part I took nothing, but there were many who made no scruple. That evening Puymartin told me Mrs. Scott's history, but it was not at all like Monsieur de Larnac's story. Roger said that, when quite little, Mrs. Scott had been stolen from her family by some acrobats, and that her father had found her in a traveling circus, riding on barebacked horses and jumping through paper hoops."

"A circus-rider!" cried Madame de Lavardens, "I should have preferred the beggar."

"And while Roger was telling me this Family Herald romance, I saw approaching from the end of a gallery a wonderful cloud of lace and satin; it surrounded this rider from a wandering circus, and I admired those shoulders, those dazzling shoulders, on which undulated a necklace of diamonds as big as the stopper of a decanter. They say that the Minister of Finance had sold secretly to Mrs. Scott half the crown diamonds, and that was how, the month before, he had been able to show a surplus of 1,500,000 francs in the budget. Add to all this that the lady had a remarkably good air, and that the little acrobat seemed perfectly at home in the midst of all this splendor."

Paul was going so far that his mother was obliged to stop him. Before M. de Larnac, who was excessively annoyed and disappointed, he showed too plainly his delight at the prospect of having this marvelous American for a near neighbor.

The Abbé Constantin was preparing to return to Longueval, but Paul, seeing him ready to start, said:

"No! no! Monsieur le Curé, you must not think of walking back to Longueval in the heat of the day. Allow me to drive you home. I am really grieved to see you so cast down, and will try my best to amuse you. Oh! if you were ten times a saint I would make you laugh at my stories."

And half an hour after, the two — the Curé and Paul — drove side by side in the direction of the village. Paul talked, talked, talked. His mother was not there to check or moderate his transports, and his joy was overflowing.

"Now, look here, Monsieur l'Abbé, you are wrong to take things in this tragic manner. Stay, look at my little mare, how well she trots! what good action she has! You have not seen her before? What do you think I paid for her? Four hundred francs. I discovered her a fortnight ago, between the shafts of a market gardener's cart. She is a treasure. I assure you she can do sixteen miles an hour, and keep one's hands full all the time. Just see how she pulls. Come, tot-tot-tot! You are not in a hurry, Monsieur l'Abbé, I hope. Let us return through the wood; the fresh air will do you good. Oh! Monsieur l'Abbé, if you only knew what a regard I have for you, and respect, too. I did not talk too much nonsense before you just now, did I? I should be so sorry —"

"No, my child, I heard nothing."

"Well, we will take the longest way round."

After having turned to the left in the wood, Paul resumed his communications.

"I was saying, Monsieur l'Abbé," he went on, "that you are wrong to take things so seriously. Shall I tell you what I think? This is a very fortunate affair."

"Very fortunate?"

"Yes, very fortunate. I would rather see the Scotts at Longueval than the Gallards. Did you not hear Monsieur de Larnac reproach these Americans with spending their money foolishly. It is never foolish to spend money. The folly lies in keeping it. Your poor for I am perfectly sure that it is your poor of whom you are thinking — your poor have made a good thing of it today. That is my opinion. The religion? Well, they will not go to mass, and that will be a grief to you, that is only natural; but they will send you money, plenty of money, and you will take it, and you will be quite right in doing so. You will see that you will not say no. There will be gold raining over the whole place; a movement, a bustle, carriages with four horses, postilions, powdered footmen, paper chases, hunting parties, balls, fireworks, and here in this very spot I shall perhaps find Paris again before long. I shall see once more the two riders, and the two little grooms of whom I was speaking just now. If you only knew how well those two sisters look on horseback! One morning I went right round the Bois de Boulogne behind them; I fancy I can see them still. They had high hats, and little black veils drawn very tightly over their faces, and long riding-habits made in the princess form, with a single seam right down the back; and a woman must be awfully well made to wear a riding-habit like that, because you see, Monsieur l'Abbé, with a habit of that cut no deception is possible."

For some moments the Curé had not been listening to Paul's discourse. They had entered a long, perfectly straight avenue, and at the end of this avenue the Curé saw a horseman galloping along.

"Look," said the Curé to Paul, "your eyes are better than mine. Is not that Jean?"

"Yes, it is jean. I know his grey mare."

Paul loved horses, and before looking at the rider looked at the horse. It was indeed Jean, who, when he saw in the distance the Curé and Paul de Lavardens, waved in the air his kepi adorned with two golden stripes. Jean was lieutenant in the regiment of artillery quartered at Souvigny.

Some moments after he stopped by the little carriage, and, addressing the Curé, said:

"I have just been to your house, *mon parrain*. Pauline told me that you had gone to Souvigny about the sale. Well, who has bought the castle?"

"An American, Mrs. Scott."

"And Blanche-Couronne?"

"The same, Mrs. Scott."

"And La Rozeraie?"

"Mrs. Scott again."

"And the forest? Mrs. Scott again?"

"You have said it," replied Paul, "and I know Mrs. Scott, and I can promise you that there will be something going on at Longueval. I will introduce you. Only it is distressing to Monsieur l'Abbé because she is an American — a Protestant."

"Ah! that is true," said Jean, sympathizingly. "However, we will talk about it tomorrow. I am going to dine with you, godfather; I have warned Pauline of my visit; no time to stop today. I am on duty, and must be in quarters at three o'clock."

"Stables?" asked Paul.

"Yes. Good-bye, Paul. Tomorrow, godfather."

The lieutenant galloped away. Paul de Lavardens gave his little horse her head.

"What a capital fellow Jean is!" said Paul.

"Oh, yes, indeed!"

"There is no one on earth better than Jean."

"No, no one."

The Curé turned round to take another look at Jean, who was almost lost in the depths of the forest.

"Oh, yes, there is you, Monsieur le Curé."

"No, not me! not me!"

"Well, Monsieur l'Abbé, shall I tell you what I think? I think there is no one better than you two — you and Jean. That is the truth, if I must tell you. Oh! what a splendid place for a trot! I shall let Niniche go; I call her Niniche."

With the point of his whip Paul caressed the flank of Niniche, who started off at full speed, and Paul, delighted, cried:

"Just look at her action, Monsieur l'Abbé! just look at her action! So regular — just like clockwork. Lean over and look."

To please Paul de Lavardens the Abbé Constantin did lean over and look at Niniche's action, but the old priest's thoughts were far away.

Chapter II

THE NEW CHATELAINE

*T*his sub-lieutenant of artillery was called Jean Reynaud. He was the son of a country doctor who slept in the churchyard of Longueval.

In 1846, when the Abbé Constantin took possession of his little living, the grandfather of Jean was residing in a pleasant cottage on the road to Souvigny, between the picturesque old castles of Longueval and Lavardens.

Marcel, the son of that Dr. Reynaud, was finishing his medical studies in Paris. He possessed great industry, and an elevation of sentiment and mind extremely rare. He passed his examinations with great distinction, and had decided to fix his abode in Paris and tempt fortune there, and everything seemed to promise him the most prosperous and brilliant career, when, in 1852, he received the news of his father's death — he had been struck down by a fit of apoplexy. Marcel hurried to Longueval, overwhelmed with grief, for he adored his father. He spent a month with his mother, and then spoke of the necessity of returning to Paris.

"That is true," said his mother; "you must go."

"What! I must go! We must go, you mean. Do you think that I would leave you here alone? I shall take you with me."

"To live in Paris; to leave the place where I was born, where your father lived, where he died? I could never do it, my child, never! Go alone; your life, your future, are there. I know you; I know that you will never forget me, that you will come and see me often, very often."

"No, mother," he answered; "I shall stay here."

And he stayed.

His hopes, his ambitions, all in one moment vanished. He saw only one thing — duty — the duty of not abandoning his aged mother. In duty, simply accepted and simply discharged, he found happiness. After all, it is only thus that one does find happiness.

Marcel bowed with courage and good grace to his new existence. He continued his father's life, entering the groove at the very spot where he had left it. He devoted himself without regret to the obscure career of a country doctor. His father had left him a little land and a little money; he lived in the most simple manner possible, and one half of his life belonged to the poor, from whom he would never receive a penny.

This was his only luxury.

He found in his way a young girl, charming, penniless, and alone in the world. He married her. This was in 1855, and the following year brought to Dr. Reynaud a great sorrow and a great joy — the death of his old mother and the birth of his son Jean.

At an interval of six weeks, the Abby Constantin recited the prayers for the dead over the grave of the grandmother, and was present in the position of godfather at the baptism of the grandson.

In consequence of constantly meeting at the bedside of the suffering and dying, the priest and the doctor had been strongly attracted to each other. They instinctively felt that they belonged to the same family, the same race — the race of the tender, the just, and the benevolent.

Year followed year — calm, peaceful, fully occupied in labor and duty. Jean was no longer an infant. His father gave him his first lessons in reading and writing, the priest his first lessons in Latin. Jean was intelligent and industrious. He made so much progress that the two professors — particularly the Curé — found themselves at the end of a few years rather cast into the shade by their pupil. It was at this moment that the Countess, after the death of her husband, came to settle at Lavardens. She brought with her a tutor for her son Paul, a very nice, but very lazy little fellow. The two children were of the same age; they had known each other from their earliest years.

Madame de Lavardens had a great regard for Dr. Reynaud, and one day she made him the following proposal:

"Send Jean to me every morning," said she, "I will send him home in the evening. Paul's tutor is a very accomplished man; he will make the children work together. It will be rendering me a real service. Jean will set Paul a good example."

Things were thus arranged, and the little bourgeois set the little nobleman a most excellent example of industry and application, but this excellent example was not followed.

The war broke out. On November 14th, at seven o'clock in the morning, the mobiles of Souvigny assembled in the great square of the town; their chaplain was the Abbé Constantin, their surgeon-major, Dr.

Reynaud. The same idea had come at the same moment to both; the priest was sixty-two, the doctor fifty.

When they started, the battalion followed the road which led through Longueval, and which passed before the doctor's house. Madame Reynaud and Jean were waiting by the roadside. The child threw himself into his father's arms.

"Take me, too, papa! take me, too!"

Madame Reynaud wept. The doctor held them both in a long embrace, then he continued his way.

A hundred steps farther the road made a sharp curve. The doctor turned, cast one long look at his wife and child-the last; he was never to see them again.

On January 8, 1871, the mobiles of Souvigny attacked the village of Villersexel, occupied by the Prussians, who had barricaded themselves. The firing began. A mobile who marched in the front rank received a ball in the chest and fell. There was a short moment of trouble and hesitation.

"Forward! forward!" shouted the officers.

The men passed over the body of their comrade, and under a hail of bullets entered the town.

Dr. Reynaud and the Abbé Constantin marched with the troops; they stopped by the wounded man; the blood was rushing in floods from his mouth.

"There is nothing to be done," said the doctor. "He is dying; he belongs to you."

The priest knelt down by the dying man, and the doctor rose to go toward the village. He had not taken ten steps when he stopped, beat the air with both hands, and fell all at once to the ground. The priest ran to him; he was dead-killed on the spot by a bullet through the temples. That evening the village was ours, and the next day they placed in the cemetery of Villersexel the body of Dr. Reynaud.

Two months later the Abbé Constantin took back to Longueval the coffin of his friend, and behind the coffin, when it was carried from the church, walked an orphan. Jean had also lost his mother. At the news of her husband's death, Madame Reynaud had remained for twenty-four hours petrified, crushed, without a word or a tear; then fever had seized her, then delirium, and after a fortnight, death.

Jean was alone in the world; he was fourteen years old. Of that family, where for more than a century all had been good and honest, there remained only a child kneeling beside a grave; but he, too, promised to be what his father and grandfather before him had been — good, and honest, and true.

There are families like that in France, and many of them, more than one ventures to say. Our poor country is in many respects calumniated by certain novelists, who draw exaggerated and distorted pictures of it. It is true the history of good people is often monotonous or painful. This story is a proof of it.

The grief of Jean was the grief of a man. He remained long sad and silent. The evening of his father's funeral the Abbé Constantin took him home to the vicarage. The day had been rainy and cold. Jean was sitting by the fireside; the priest was reading his breviary opposite him. Old Pauline came and went, arranging her affairs.

An hour passed without a word, when Jean, raising his head, said:

"Godfather, did my father leave me any money?"

This question was so extraordinary that the old priest, stupefied, could scarcely believe that he heard aright.

"You ask if your father —"

"I asked if my father left me some money?"

"Yes; he must have left you some."

"A good deal, don't you think? I have often heard people say that my father was rich. Tell me about how much he has left me!"

"But I don't know. You ask —"

The poor old man felt his heart rent in twain. Such a question at such a moment! Yet he thought he knew the boy's heart, and in that heart there should not be room for such thoughts.

"Pray, dear godfather, tell me," continued Jean, gently. "I will explain to you afterward why I ask that."

"Well, they say your father had 200,000 or 300,000 francs."

"And is that much?"

"Yes, it is a great deal."

"And it is all mine?"

"Yes, it is all yours."

"Oh! I am glad, because, you know, the day that my father was killed in the war, the Prussians killed, at the same time, the son of a poor woman in Longueval — old Clemence, you know; and they killed, too, the brother of Rosalie, with whom I used to play when I was quite little. Well, since I am rich and they are poor, I will divide with Clemence and Rosalie the money my father has left me."

On hearing these words the Curé rose, took Jean by both hands, and drew him into his arms. The white head rested on the fair one. Two large tears escaped from the eyes of the old priest, rolled slowly down his cheeks, and were lost in the furrows of his face.

However, the Curé was obliged to explain to Jean that, though he was his father's heir, he had not the right of disposing of his heritage as he would. There would be a family council, and a guardian would be appointed.

"You, no doubt, godfather?"

"No, not I, my child; a priest has not the right of exercising the functions of a guardian. They will, I think, choose Monsieur Lenient, the lawyer in Souvigny, who was one of your father's best friends. You can speak to him and tell him what you wish."

M. Lenient was eventually appointed guardian, and Jean urged his wishes so eagerly and touchingly that the lawyer consented to deduct from the income a sum of 2,400 francs, which, every year till Jean came of age, was divided between old Clemence and little Rosalie.

Under these circumstances, Madame de Lavardens was perfect. She went to the Abbé and said:

"Give Jean to me, give him to me entirely till he has finished his studies. I will bring him back to you every year during the holidays. It is not I who am rendering you a service; it is a service which I ask of you. I cannot imagine any greater good fortune for my son than to have Jean for a companion. I must resign myself to leaving Lavardens for a time. Paul is bent upon being a soldier and going up to Saint-Cyr. It is only in Paris that I can obtain the necessary masters. I will take the two children there; they will study together under my own eyes like brothers, and I will make no difference between them; of that you may be sure."

It was difficult to refuse such an offer. The old Curé would have dearly liked to keep Jean with him, and his heart was torn at the thought of this separation, but what was for the child's real interest? That was the only question to be considered; the rest was nothing. They summoned Jean.

"My child," said Madame de Lavardens to him, "will you come and live with Paul and me for some years? I will take you both to Paris."

"You are very kind, Madame, but I should have liked so much to stay here."

He looked at the Curé, who turned away his eyes.

"Why must we go?" he continued. "Why must you take Paul and me away?"

"Because it is only in Paris that you can have all the advantages necessary to complete your studies. Paul will prepare for his examination at Saint-Cyr. You know he wishes to be a soldier."

"So do I, Madame. I wish to be one, too."

"You a soldier!" exclaimed the Curé; "but you know that was not at all your father's idea. In my presence, he has often spoken of your future, your career. You were to be a doctor, and, like him, doctor at Longueval, and, like him, devote yourself to the sick and poor. Jean, my child, do you remember?"

"I remember, I remember."

"Well, then, Jean, you must do as your father wished; it is your duty, Jean; it is your duty. You must go to Paris. You would like to stay here, I understand that well, and I should like it, too; but it can not be. You must go to Paris, and work, work hard. Not that I am anxious about that; you are your father's true son. You will be an honest and laborious man. One can not well be the one without the other. And some day, in your father's house, in the place where he has done so much good, the poor people of the country round will find another Doctor Reynaud, to whom they may look for help. And I — if by chance I am still in this world — when that day comes, I shall be so happy! But I am wrong to speak of myself; I ought not, I do not count. It is of your father that you must think. I repeat it, Jean, it was his dearest wish. You can not have forgotten it."

"No, I have not forgotten; but if my father sees me, and hears me, I am certain that he understands and forgives me, for it is on his account."

"On his account?"

"Yes. When I heard that he was dead, and when I heard how he died, all at once, without any need of reflection, I said to myself that I would be a soldier, and I will be a soldier! Godfather, and you, Madame, I beg you not to prevent me."

The child burst into tears — a perfect flood of passionate tears. The Countess and the Abbé soothed him with gentle words.

"Yes — yes — it is settled," they said; "anything that you wish, all that you wish."

Both had the same thought — leave it to time; Jean is only a child; he will change his mind.

In this, both were mistaken; Jean did not change his mind. In the month of September, 1876, Paul de Lavardens was rejected at Saint-Cyr, and Jean Reynaud passed eleventh at the École Polytechnique. The day when the list of the candidates who had passed was published, he wrote to the Abbé Constantin:

"I have passed, and passed too well, for I wish to go into the army, and not the civil service; however, if I keep my place in the school, that will be the business of one of my comrades; he will have my chance."

It happened so in the end. Jean Reynaud did better than keep his place; the pass-list showed his name seventh, but instead of entering *l'École des Ponts et Chaussees,* he entered the military college at Fontainebleau in 1878.

He was then just twenty-one; he was of age, master of his fortune, and the first act of the new administration was a great, a very great piece of extravagance.

He bought for old Clemence and little Rosalie two shares in Government stock of 1,500 francs each. That cost him 70,000 francs, almost the sum that Paul de Lavardens, in his first year of liberty in Paris, spent for Mademoiselle Lise Bruyere, of the Palais Royal Théâtre.

Two years later Jean passed first at the examination, and left Fontainebleau with the right of choosing among the vacant places. There was one in the regiment quartered at Souvigny, and Souvigny was three miles from Longueval. Jean asked for this, and obtained it.

Thus Jean Reynaud, lieutenant in the ninth regiment of artillery, came in the month of October, 1880, to take possession of the house that had been his father's; thus he found himself once more in the place where his childhood had passed, and where everyone had kept green the memory of the life and death of his father; thus the Abbé Constantin was not denied the happiness of once again having near him the son of his old friend, and, if the truth must be told, he no longer wished that Jean had become a doctor.

When the old Curé left his church after saying mass, when he saw coming along the road a great cloud of dust, when he felt the earth tremble under the rumbling cannon, he would stop, and, like a child, amuse himself with seeing the regiment pass, but to him the regiment was — Jean. It was this robust and manly cavalier, in whose face, as in an open book, one read uprightness, courage, and goodness.

The moment Jean perceived the Curé, he would put his horse to a gallop, and go to have a little chat with his godfather. The horse would turn his head toward the Curé, for he knew very well there was always a piece of sugar for him in the pocket of that old black soutane — rusty and worn — the morning soutane. The Abbé Constantin had a beautiful new one, of which he took great care, to wear in society — when he went into society.

The trumpets of the regiment sounded as they passed through the village, and all eyes sought Jean — "little Jean"-for to the old people of Longueval he was still little Jean. Certain wrinkled, broken-down, old peasants had never been able to break themselves of the habit of saluting him when he passed with, "Bonjour, gamin, ca va bien?"

He was six feet high, this gamin, and Jean never crossed the village without perceiving at one window the old furrowed parchment skin of Clemence, and at another the smiling countenance of Rosalie. The latter had married during the previous year; Jean had given her away, and joyously on the wedding-night had he danced with the girls of Longueval.

Such was the lieutenant of artillery, who, on Saturday, May 28, 1881, at half-past four in the afternoon, sprang from his horse before the door of the vicarage of Longueval. He entered the gate, the horse obediently followed, and went by himself into a little shed in the yard. Pauline was at the kitchen window; Jean approached and kissed her heartily on both cheeks.

"Good-evening, Pauline. Is all well?"

"Very well. I am busy preparing your dinner; would you like to know what you are going to have? potato soup, a leg of mutton, and a custard."

"That is excellent; I shall enjoy everything, for I am dying of hunger."

"And a salad; I had forgotten it; you can help me cut it directly. Dinner will be at half-past six exactly, for at half-past seven Monsieur le Curé has his service for the month of Mary."

"Where is my godfather?"

"You will find him in the garden. He is very sad on account of this sale of yesterday."

"Yes, I know, I know."

"It will cheer him a little to see you; he is always so happy when you are here. Take care; Loulou is going to eat the climbing roses. How hot he is!"

"I came the long way by the wood, and rode very fast."

Jean captured Loulou, who was directing his steps toward the climbing roses. He unsaddled him, fastened him in the little shed, rubbed him down with a great handful of straw, after which he entered the house, relieved himself of his sword and kepi, replaced the latter by an old straw hat, value sixpence, and then went to look for his godfather in the garden.

The poor Abbé was indeed sad; he had scarcely closed an eye all night — he who generally slept so easily, so quietly, the sound sleep of a child. His soul was wrung. Longueval in the hands of a foreigner, of a heretic, of an adventuress!

Jean repeated what Paul had said the evening before.

"You will have money, plenty of money, for your poor."

"Money! money! Yes, my poor will not lose, perhaps they will even gain by it; but I must go and ask for this money, and in the salon, instead of my old and dear friend, I shall find this red-haired American. It seems that she has red hair! I will certainly go for the sake of my poor — I will go — and she will give me the money, but she will give me nothing but money; the Marquise gave me something else — her life and her heart. Every week we went together to visit the sick and the poor;

she knew all the sufferings and the miseries of the country round, and when the gout nailed me to my easy chair she made the rounds alone, and as well, or better than I."

Pauline interrupted this conversation. She carried an immense earthenware salad-dish, on which bloomed, violent and startling, enormous red flowers.

"Here I am," said Pauline, "I am going to cut the salad. Jean, would you like lettuce or endive?"

"Endive," said Jean, gaily. "It is a long time since I have had any endive."

"Well, you shall have some tonight. Stay, take the dish."

Pauline began to cut the endive, and Jean bent down to receive the leaves in the great salad dish. The Curé looked on.

At this moment a sound of little bells was heard. A carriage was approaching; one heard the jangling and creaking of its wheels. The Curé's little garden was only separated from the road by a low hedge, in the middle of which was a little trellised gate.

All three looked out, and saw driving down the road a hired carriage of most primitive construction, drawn by two great white horses, and driven by an old coachman in a blouse. Beside this old coachman was seated a tall footman in livery, of the most severe and correct demeanor. In the carriage were two young women, dressed both alike in very elegant, but very simple, traveling costumes.

When the carriage was opposite the gate the coachman stopped his horses, and addressing the Abbé:

"Monsieur le Curé," said he, "these ladies wish to speak to you."

Then, turning toward the ladies:

"This is Monsieur le Curé of Longueval."

The Abbé Constantin approached and opened the little gate. The travelers alighted. Their looks rested, not without astonishment, on the young officer, who stood there, a little embarrassed, with his straw hat in one hand, and his salad dish, all overflowing with endive, in the other.

The visitors entered the garden, and the elder — she seemed about twenty-five — addressing the Abbé Constantin, said to him, with a little foreign accent, very original and very peculiar:

"I am obliged to introduce myself — Mrs. Scott; I am Mrs. Scott! It was I who bought the castle and farms and all the rest here at the sale yesterday. I hope that I do not disturb you, and that you can spare me five minutes." Then, pointing to her traveling companion, "Miss Bettina Percival, my sister; you guessed it, I am sure. We are very much alike, are we not? Ah! Bettina, we have left our bags in the carriage, and we shall want them directly."

"I will get them."

And as Miss Percival prepared to go for the two little bags, Jean said to her:

"Pray allow me."

"I am really very sorry to give you so much trouble. The servant will give them to you; they are on the front seat."

She had the same accent as her sister, the same large eyes — black, laughing, and gay-and the same hair, not red, but fair, with golden shades, where daintily danced the light of the sun. She bowed to Jean with a pretty little smile, and he, having returned to Pauline the salad dish full of endive, went to look for the two little bags. Meanwhile-much agitated, sorely disturbed — the Abbé Constantin introduced into his vicarage the new Chatelaine of Longueval.

Chapter III

DELIGHTFUL SURPRISES

*T*his vicarage of Longueval was far from being a palace. The same apartment on the ground floor served for dining and drawing room, communicating directly with the kitchen by a door, which stood always wide open. This room was furnished in the most scanty manner; two old armchairs, six straw chairs, a sideboard, a round table. Pauline had already laid the cloth for the dinner of the Abbé and Jean.

Mrs. Scott and Miss Percival went and came, examining the domestic arrangements of the Curé with a sort of childish wonder.

"But the garden, the house, everything is charming," said Mrs. Scott.

They both boldly penetrated into the kitchen; the Abbé Constantin followed them, scared, bewildered, stupefied at the suddenness and resolution of this American invasion.

Old Pauline, with an anxious and gloomy air, examined the two foreigners.

"There they are, then," she said to herself, "these Protestants, these accursed heretics!"

"I must compliment you," said Bettina; "it is so beautifully kept. Look, Susie, is not the vicarage altogether exactly what you wished?"

"And so is the Curé," rejoined Mrs. Scott. "Yes, Monsieur le Curé, if you will permit me to say so, you do not know how happy it makes me to find you just what you are. In the railway carriage what did I say to you, Bettina? And again just now, when we were driving here?"

"My sister said to me, Monsieur le Curé, that what she desired above everything was a priest, not young, or melancholy, or severe; but one with white hair and a kind and gentle manner. And that is exactly what you are, Monsieur le Curé, exactly. No, we could not have been more fortunate. Excuse me for speaking to you in this manner; the Parisians know how to make pretty phrases, but I do not, and in speaking French I should often be quite at a loss if I did not say everything in a simple and childish way, as it comes into my head. In a word, I am satisfied, quite satisfied, and I hope that you, too, Monsieur le Curé, will be as satisfied with your new parishioners."

"My parishioners!" exclaimed the Curé, all at once recovering speech, movement, life, everything which for some moments had completely abandoned him. "My parishioners! Pardon me, Madame, Mademoiselle, I am so agitated. You will be — you are Catholics?"

"Certainly we are Catholics."

"Catholics! Catholics!" repeated the Curé.

"Catholics! Catholics!" echoed old Pauline.

Mrs. Scott looked from the Curé to Pauline, from Pauline to the Curé, much surprised that a single word should produce such an effect, and, to complete the tableau, Jean appeared carrying the two little traveling bags.

The Curé and Pauline saluted him with the same words:

"Catholics! Catholics!"

"Ah! I begin to understand," said Mrs. Scott, laughing. "It is our name, our country; you must have thought that we were Protestants. Not at all. Our mother was a Canadian, French and Catholic by descent; that is why my sister and I both speak French, with an accent, it is true, and with certain American idioms, but yet in such a manner as to be able to express nearly all we want to say. My husband is a Protestant, but he allows me complete liberty, and my two children are Catholics. That is why, Monsieur l'Abbé, we wished to come and see you the very first day."

"That is one reason," continued Bettina, "but there is also another; but for that reason we shall want our little bags."

"Here they are," said Jean.

While the two little bags passed from the hands of the officer to those of Mrs. Scott and Bettina, the Curé introduced Jean to the two Americans, but his agitation was so great that the introduction was not made strictly according to rule. The Curé only forgot one thing, it is true, but that was a thing tolerably essential in an introduction — the family name of Jean.

"It is Jean," said he, "my godson, lieutenant of artillery, now quartered at Souvigny. He is one of the family."

Jean made two deep bows, the Americans two little ones, after which they foraged in their bags, from which each drew a *rouleau* of 1,000 francs, daintily enclosed in green sheaths of serpent-skin, clasped with gold.

"I have brought you this for your poor," said Mrs. Scott.

"And I have brought this," said Bettina.

"And besides that, Monsieur le Curé, I am going to give you five hundred francs a month," said Mrs. Scott.

"And I will do like my sister."

Delicately they slipped their offerings into the right and left hands of the Curé, who, looking at each hand alternately, said:

"What are these little things? They are very heavy; there must be money in them. Yes, but how much, how much?"

The Abbé Constantin was seventy-two, and much money had passed through his hands, but this money had come to him in small sums, and the idea of such an offering as this had never entered his head. Two thousand francs! Never had he had so much in his possession — no, not even one thousand. He stammered:

"I am very grateful to you, Madame; you are very good, Mademoiselle —"

But after all he could not thank them enough, and Jean thought it necessary to come to his assistance.

"They have given you two thousand francs!"

And then, full of warmest gratitude; the Curé cried:

"Two thousand francs! Two thousand francs for my poor!"

Pauline suddenly reappeared.

"Here, Pauline," said the Curé, "put away this money, and take care —"

Old Pauline filled many positions in this simple household: cook, maid-of-all-work, treasurer, dispenser. Her hands received with a respectful tremble these two little *rouleaux* which represented so much misery alleviated, so much suffering relieved.

"One thousand francs a month! But there will be no poor left in the country."

"That is just what I wish. I am rich, very rich, and so is my sister; she is even richer than I am, because a young girl has not so many expenses, while I — Ah! well, I spend all that I can — all that I can. When one has a great deal of money, too much, more than one feels to be just, tell me, Monsieur le Curé, is there any other way of obtaining pardon than to keep one's hands open, and give, give, give, all one can, and as usefully as one can? Besides, you can give me something in return;" and, turning to Pauline, "Will you be so kind as to give me a glass of water? No, nothing else; a glass of cold water; I am dying of thirst."

"And I," said Bettina, laughing, while Pauline ran to fetch the water, "I am dying of something else-of hunger, to tell the truth. Monsieur le Curé — I know that I am going to be dreadfully intrusive; I see your cloth is laid — could you not invite us to dinner?"

"Bettina!" said Mrs. Scott.

"Let me alone, Susie, let me alone. Won't you, Monsieur le Curé? I am sure you will."

But he could find no reply. The old Curé hardly knew where he was. They had taken his vicarage by storm; they were Catholics; they had promised him one thousand francs a month, and now they wanted to dine with him. Ah! that was the last stroke. Terror seized him at the thought of having to do the honors of his leg of mutton and his custard to these two absurdly rich Americans. He murmured:

"Dine!-you would like to dine here?"

Jean thought he must interpose again. "It would be a great pleasure to my godfather," said he, "if you would kindly stay. But I know what disturbs him. We were going to dine together, just the two of us, and you must not expect a feast. You will be very indulgent?"

"Yes, yes, very indulgent," replied Bettina; then, addressing her sister, "Come, Susie, you must not be cross, because I have been a little — you know it is my way to be a little — Let us stay, will you? It will do us good to pass a quiet hour here, after such a day as we have had! On the railway, in the carriage, in the heat, in the dust; we had such a horrid luncheon, in such a horrid hotel. We were to have returned to the same hotel at seven o'clock to dine, and then take the train back to Paris, but dinner here will be really much nicer. You won't say no? Ah! how good you are, Susie!"

She embraced her sister fondly; then turning toward the Curé:

"If you only knew, Monsieur le Curé, how good she is!"

"Bettina! Bettina!"

"Come," said Jean, "quick, Pauline, two more plates; I will help you."

"And so will I," said Bettina, "I will help, too. Oh! do let me; it will be so amusing. Monsieur le Curé, you will let me do a little as if I were at home?"

In a moment she had taken off her mantle, and Jean could admire, in all its exquisite perfection, a figure marvelous for suppleness and grace. Miss Percival then removed her hat, but with a little too much haste, for this was the signal for a charming catastrophe. A whole avalanche descended in torrents, in long cascades, over Bettina's shoulders. She was standing before a window flooded by the rays of the sun, and this golden light, falling full on this golden hair, formed a delicious frame for the sparkling beauty of the young girl. Confused and blushing, Bettina was obliged to call her sister to her aid, and Mrs. Scott had much trouble in introducing order into this disorder.

When this disaster was at length repaired, nothing could prevent Bettina from rushing on plates, knives, and forks.

"Oh, indeed," said she to Jean, "I know very well how to lay the cloth. Ask my sister. Tell him, Susie, when I was a little girl in New York, I used to lay the cloth very well, didn't I?"

"Very well, indeed," said Mrs. Scott.

And then, while begging the Curé to excuse Bettina's want of thought, she, too, took off her hat and mantle, so that Jean had again the very agreeable spectacle of a charming figure and beautiful hair; but, to Jean's great regret, the catastrophe had not a second representation.

In a few minutes Mrs. Scott, Miss Percival, the Curé, and Jean were seated round the little vicarage table; then, thanks partly to the impromptu and original nature of the entertainment, partly to the good-humor and perhaps slightly audacious gayety of Bettina, the conversation took a turn of the frankest and most cordial familiarity.

"Now, Monsieur le Curé," said Bettina, "you shall see if I did not speak the truth when I said I was dying of hunger. I never was so glad to sit down to dinner. This is such a delightful finish to our day. Both my sister and I are perfectly happy now we have this castle, and these farms, and the forest."

"And then," said Mrs. Scott, "to have all that in such an extraordinary and unexpected manner. We were so taken by surprise."

"You may indeed say so, Susie. You must know, Monsieur l'Abbé, that yesterday was my sister's birthday. But first, pardon me, Monsieur — Jean, is it not?"

"Yes, Miss Percival, Monsieur Jean."

"Well, Monsieur Jean, a little more of that excellent soup, if you please."

The Abbé was beginning to recover a little, but he was still too agitated to perform the duties of a host. It was Jean who had undertaken the management of his godfather's little dinner. He filled the plate of the charming American, who fixed upon him the glance of two large eyes, in which sparkled frankness, daring, and gayety. The eyes of Jean, meanwhile, repaid Miss Percival in the same coin. It was scarcely three quarters of an hour since the young American and the young officer had made acquaintance in the Curé's garden, yet both felt already perfectly at ease with each other, full of confidence, almost like old friends.

"I told you, Monsieur l'Abbé," continued Bettina, "that yesterday was my sister's birthday. A week ago my brother-in-law was obliged to return to America, but at starting he said to my sister, 'I shall not be with you on your birthday, but you will hear from me.' So, yesterday, presents and bouquets arrived from all quarters, but from my brother-in-law, up to five o'clock, nothing — nothing. We were just starting for a ride in the Bois, and *a propos* of riding" — she stopped, and looking curiously at Jean's great dusty boots — "Monsieur Jean, you have spurs on."

"Yes, Miss Percival."

"Then you are in the cavalry?"

"I am in the artillery, and that, you know, is cavalry."

"And your regiment is quartered?" —

"Quite near here."

"Then you will be able to ride with us?"

"With the greatest pleasure."

"That is settled. Let me see; where was I?"

"You do not know at all where you are, Bettina, and you are telling these gentlemen things which can not interest them."

"Oh! I beg your pardon," said the Curé. "The sale of this estate is the only subject of conversation in the neighborhood just now, and Miss Percival's account interests me very much."

"You see, Susie, my account interests Monsieur le Curé very much; then I shall continue. We went for our ride, we returned at seven o'clock — nothing. We dined, and just when we were leaving the table a telegram from America arrived. It contained only a few lines:

"'I have ordered the purchase today, for you and in your name, of the castle and lands of Longueval, near Souvigny, on the Northern Railway line.'

"Then we both burst into a fit of wild laughter at the thought."

"No, no, Bettina; you calumniate us both. Our first thought was one of very sincere gratitude, for both my sister and I are very fond of the country. My husband knows that we had longed to have an estate in France. For six months he had been looking out, and found nothing. At last he discovered this one, and, without telling us, ordered it to be bought for my birthday. It was a delicate attention."

"Yes, Susie, you are right, but after the little fit of gratitude, we had a great one of gayety."

"Yes, I confess it. When we realized that we had suddenly become possessed of a castle, without knowing in the least where it was, what it was like, or how much it had cost, it seemed so like a fairy-tale. Well, for five good minutes we laughed with all our hearts, then we seized the map of France, and succeeded in discovering Souvigny. When he had finished with the map it was the turn of the railway guide, and this morning, by the ten o'clock express, we arrived at Souvigny.

"We have passed the whole day in visiting the castle, the farms, the woods, the stables. We are delighted with what we have seen. Only, Monsieur le Curé, there is one thing about which I feel curious. I know that the place was sold yesterday; but I have not dared to ask either agent or farmer who accompanied me in my walk — for my ignorance would have seemed too absurd — I have not dared to ask how much it cost. In the telegram my husband does not mention the sum. Since I am so delighted with the place, the price is only a detail, but still I should like to know it. Tell me, Monsieur le Curé, do you know what it cost?"

"An enormous price," replied the Curé, "for many hopes and many ambitions were excited about Longueval."

"An enormous price! You frighten me. How much exactly?"

"Three millions!"

"Is that all? Is that all?" cried Mrs. Scott. "The castle, the farms, the forest, all for three millions?"

"But that is nothing," said Bettina. "That delicious little stream which wanders through the park is alone worth three millions."

"And you said just now, Monsieur le Curé, that there were several persons who disputed the purchase with us?"

"Yes, Mrs. Scott."

"And, after the sale, was my name mentioned among these persons?"

"Certainly it was."

"And when my name was mentioned was there no one there who spoke of me? Yes, yes, your silence is a sufficient answer; they did speak of me. Well, Monsieur le Curé, I am now serious, very serious. I beg you as a favor to tell me what was said."

"But," replied the poor Curé, who felt himself upon burning coals, "they spoke of your large fortune."

"Yes, of course, they would be obliged to speak of that, and no doubt they said that I was very rich, but had not been rich long — that I was a parvenu. Very well, but that is not all; they must have said something else."

"No, indeed; I have heard nothing else."

"Oh, Monsieur le Curé, that is what you may call a white lie, and it is making you very unhappy, because naturally you are the soul of truth; but if I torment you thus it is because I have the greatest interest in knowing what was said."

"You are right," interrupted Jean, "you are right. They said you were one of the most elegant, the most brilliant, and the —"

"And one of the prettiest women in Paris. With a little indulgence they might say that; but that is not all yet — there is something else."

"Oh! I assure you —"

"Yes, there is something else, and I should like to hear it this very moment, and I should like the information to be very frank and very exact. It seems to me that I am in a lucky vein today, and I feel as if you were both a little inclined to be my friends, and that you will be so entirely some day. Well, tell me if I am right in supposing that should false and absurd stories be told about me you will help me to contradict them."

"Yes!" replied Jean, "you are right in believing that."

"Well, then, it is to you that I address myself. You are a soldier, and courage is part of your profession. Promise me to be brave. Will you promise me?"

"What do you understand by being brave?"

"Promise, promise — without explanations, without conditions."

"Well, I promise."

"You will then reply frankly, 'Yes' or 'No,' to questions?"

"I will."

"Did they say that I had begged in the streets of New York?"

"Yes, they said so."

"Did they say I had been a rider in a traveling circus?"

"Yes; they said that, too."

"Very well; that is plain speaking. Now remark first that in all this there is nothing that one might not acknowledge if it were true; but it is not true, and have I not the right of denying it? My history — I will tell it you in a few words. I am going to pass a part of my life in this place, and I desire that all should know who I am and whence I come. To begin, then. Poor! Yes, I have been, and very poor. Eight years ago my father died, and was soon followed by my mother. I was then eighteen, and Bettina nine. We were alone in the world, encumbered with heavy debts and a great lawsuit. My father's last words had been, 'Susie, never, never compromise. Millions, my children, you will have millions.' He embraced us both; soon delirium seized him, and he died repeating, 'Millions; millions!' The next morning a lawyer appeared, who offered to pay all our debts, and to give us besides ten thousand dollars, if we would give up all our claims. I refused. It was then that for several months we were very poor."

"And it was then," said Bettina, "that I used to lay the cloth."

"I spent my life among the solicitors of New York, but no one would take up my case; everywhere I received the same reply: 'Your cause is very doubtful; you have rich and formidable adversaries; you need money, large sums of money, to bring such a case to a conclusion, and you have nothing. They offer to pay your debts, and to give you ten thousand dollars besides. Accept it, and sell your case.' But my father's last words rang in my ears, and I would not. Poverty, however, might soon have forced me to, when one day I made another attempt on one of my father's old friends, a banker in New York, Mr. William Scott. He was not alone; a young man was sitting in his office.

"'You may speak freely,' said Mr. Scott; 'it is my son Richard.'

"I looked at the young man, he looked at me, and we recognized each other.

"'Susie!'

"'Richard!'"

"Formerly, as children, we had often played together and were great friends. Seven or eight years before this meeting he had been sent to Europe to finish his education. We shook hands; his father made me sit down, and asked what had brought me. He listened to my tale; and replied:

"'You would require twenty or thirty thousand dollars. No one would lend you such a sum upon the uncertain chances of a very complicated lawsuit. If you are in difficulties; if you need assistance —'

"'It is not that, father. That is not what Miss Percival asks.'

"'I know that very well, but what she asks is impossible.'

"He rose to let me out. Then the sense of my helplessness overpowered me for the first time since my father's death. I burst into a violent flood of tears. An hour later Richard Scott was with me.

"'Susie,' he said, 'promise to accept what I am going to offer.'

"I promised him.

"'Well,' said he, 'on the single condition that my father shall know nothing about it, I place at your disposal the necessary sum.'

"'But then you ought to know what the lawsuit is — what it is worth.'

"'I do not know a single word about it, and I do not wish to. Besides, you have promised to accept it; you can not withdraw now.'

"I accepted. Three months after the case was ours. All this vast property became beyond dispute the property of Bettina and me. The other side offered to buy it of us for five million dollars. I consulted Richard.

"'Refuse it and wait,' said he; 'if they offer you such a sum it is because the property is worth double.'

"'However, I must return you your money; I owe you a great deal.'

"'Oh! as for that there is no hurry; I am very easy about it; my money is quite safe now.'

"'But I should like to pay you at once. I have a horror of debt! Perhaps there is another way without selling the property. Richard, will you be my husband?'

"Yes, Monsieur le Curé, yes," said Mrs. Scott, laughing, "it is thus that I threw myself at my husband's head. It is I who asked his hand. But really I was obliged to act thus. Never, never, would he have spoken; I had become too rich, and as it was me he loved, and not my money, he was becoming terribly afraid of me. That is the history of my marriage. As to the history of my fortune, it can be told in a few words. There were indeed millions in those wide lands of Colorado; they discovered there abundant mines of silver, and from those mines we draw every year an income which is beyond reason, but we have agreed — my husband, my sister, and myself — to give a very large share of this income to the poor. You see, Monsieur le Curé, it is because we have known very hard times that you will always find us ready to help those who are, as we have been ourselves, involved in the difficulties and sorrows of life. And now, Monsieur Jean, will you forgive me this long discourse, and offer me a little of that cream, which looks so very good?"

This cream was Pauline's custard, and while Jean was serving Mrs. Scott:

"I have not yet finished," she continued. "You ought to know what gave rise to these extravagant stories. A year ago, when we settled in Paris, we considered it our duty on our arrival to give a certain sum to the poor. Who was it spoke of that? None of us, certainly, but the thing was told in a newspaper, with the amount. Immediately two young reporters hastened to subject Mr. Scott to a little examination on his past history; they wished to give a sketch of our career in the — what do you call them? — society papers. Mr. Scott is sometimes a little hasty; he was so on this occasion, and dismissed these gentlemen rather brusquely, without telling them anything. So, as they did not know our real history, they invented one, and certainly displayed a very lively imagination. First they related how I had begged in the snow in New York; the next day appeared a still more sensational article, which made me a rider in a circus in Philadelphia. You have some very funny papers in France; so have we in America, for the matter of that."

During the last five minutes, Pauline had been making desperate signs to the Curé, who persisted in not understanding them, till at last the poor woman, calling up all her courage, said:

"Monsieur le Curé, it is a quarter past seven."

"A quarter past seven! Ladies, I must beg you to excuse me. This evening I have the special service for the month of Mary."

"The month of Mary? And will the service begin directly?"

"Yes, directly."

"And when does our train start for Paris?"

"At half past nine," replied Jean.

"Susie, can we not go to church first?"

"Yes, we will go," replied Mrs. Scott; "but before we separate, Monsieur le Curé, I have one favor to ask you. I should like very much, the first time I dine at Longueval, that you would dine with me, and you, too,

Monsieur Jean, just us four alone like today. Oh! do not refuse my invitation; it is given with all my heart."

"And accepted as heartily," replied Jean.

"I will write and tell you the day, and it shall be as soon as possible. You call that having a housewarming, don't you? Well, we shall have the house-warming all to ourselves."

Meanwhile, Pauline had drawn Miss Percival into a corner of the room, and was talking to her with great animation. The conversation ended with these words:

"You will be there?" said Bettina, "and you will tell me the exact moment?"

"I will tell you, but take care. Here is Monsieur le Curé; he must not suspect anything."

The two sisters, the Curé, and Jean left the house. To go to the church they were obliged to cross the churchyard. The evening was delicious. Slowly, silently, under the rays of the setting sun, the four walked down a long avenue.

On their way was the monument to Dr. Reynaud, very simple, but which, by its fine proportions, showed distinctly among the other tombs.

Mrs. Scott and Bettina stopped, struck with this inscription carved on the stone:

"Here lies Dr. Marcel Reynaud, Surgeon-Major of the Souvigny Mobiles; killed January 8, 1871, at the Battle of Villersexel. Pray for him."

When they had read it, the Curé, pointing to Jean, said:

"It was his father!"

The two sisters drew near the tomb, and with bent heads remained there for some minutes, pensive, touched, contemplative. Then both turned, and at the same moment, by the same impulse, offered their hands to Jean; then continued their walk to the church. Their first prayer at Longueval had been for the father of Jean.

The Curé went to put on his surplice and stole. Jean conducted Mrs. Scott to the seat which belonged to the masters of Longueval.

Pauline had gone on before. She was waiting for Miss Percival in the shadow behind one of the pillars. By a steep and narrow staircase, she led Bettina to the gallery, and placed her before the harmonium.

Preceded by two little chorister boys, the old Curé left the vestry, and at the moment when he knelt on the steps of the alter:

"Now! Mademoiselle," said Pauline, whose heart beat with impatience. "Poor, dear man, how pleased he will be."

When he heard the sound of the music rise, soft as a murmur, and spread through the little church, the Abbé Constantin was filled with such emotion, such joy, that the tears came to his eyes. He could not remember having wept since the day when Jean had said that he wished to share all that he possessed with the mother and sister of those who had fallen by his father's side under the Prussian bullets.

To bring tears to the eyes of the old priest, a little American had been brought across the seas to play a reverie of Chopin in the little church of Longueval.

Chapter IV

A RIOT OF CHARITY

*T*he next day, at half-past five in the morning, the bugle-call rang through the barrack-yard at Souvigny. Jean mounted his horse, and took his place with his division. By the end of May all the recruits in the army are sufficiently instructed to be capable of sharing in the general evolutions. Almost every day maneuvers of the mounted artillery are executed on the parade-ground. Jean loved his profession; he was in the habit of inspecting carefully the grooming and harness of the horses, the equipment and carriage of his men. This morning, however, he bestowed but scant attention on all the little details of his duty.

One problem agitated, tormented him, and left him always undecided, and this problem was one of those the solution of which is not given at the École Polytechnique. Jean could find no convincing reply to this question: Which of the two sisters is the prettier?

At the butts, during the first part of the maneuver, each battery worked on its own account, under the orders of the captain; but he often relinquished the place to one of his lieutenants, in order to accustom them to the management of six field-pieces. It happened on this day that the command was entrusted to the hands of Jean. To the great surprise of the Captain, in whose estimation his Lieutenant held the first rank as a well-trained, smart, and capable officer, everything went wrong. The Captain was obliged to interfere; he addressed a little reprimand to Jean, which terminated in these words:

"I can not understand it at all. What is the matter with you this morning? It is the first time such a thing has happened with you."

It was also the first time that Jean had seen anything at the butts at Souvigny but cannon, ammunition wagons, horses, or gunners.

In the clouds of dust raised by the wheels of the wagons and the hoofs of the horses Jean beheld, not the second mounted battery of the 9th Regiment of artillery, but the distinct images of two Americans with

black eyes and golden hair; and, at the moment when he listened
respectfully to the well-merited lecture from his Captain, he was in the
act of saying to himself:

"The prettier is Mrs. Scott!"

Every morning the exercise is divided into two parts by a little interval
of ten minutes. The officers gathered together and talked; Jean remained
apart, alone with his recollections of the previous evening. His thoughts
obstinately gathered round the vicarage of Longueval.

"Yes! the more charming of the two sisters is Mrs. Scott; Miss Percival
is only a child."

He saw again Mrs. Scott at the Curé's little table. He heard her story
told with such frankness, such freedom. The harmony of that very
peculiar, very fascinating voice, still enchanted his ear. He was again in
the church; she was there before him, bending over her prie-Dieu, her
pretty head resting in her two little hands; then the music arose, and far
off, in the dusk, Jean perceived the fine and delicate profile of Bettina.

"A child — is she only a child?"

The trumpets sounded, the practice was resumed; this time, fortu-
nately, no command, no responsibility. The four batteries executed their
evolutions together; this immense mass of men, horses, and carriages,
deployed in every direction, now drawn out in a long line, again
collected into a compact group. All stopped at the same instant along
the whole extent of the ground; the gunners sprang from their horses,
ran to their pieces, detached each from its team, which went off at a trot
and prepared to fire with amazing rapidity. Then the horses returned,
the men re-attached their pieces; sprang quickly to saddle, and the
regiment started at full gallop across the field.

Very gently in the thoughts of Jean Bettina regained her advantage
over Mrs. Scott. She appeared to him smiling and blushing amid the
sunlit clouds of her floating hair. Monsieur Jean, she had called him,
Monsieur Jean, and never had his name sounded so sweet. And that last
pressure of the hand on taking leave, before entering the carriage. Had
not Miss Percival given him a more cordial clasp than Mrs. Scott had
done? Yes, positively a little more.

"I was mistaken," thought Jean; "the prettier is Miss Percival."

The day's work was finished; the pieces were ranged regularly in line
one behind the other; they defiled rapidly, with a horrible clatter, and
in a cloud of dust. When Jean, sword in hand, passed before his Colonel,
the images of the two sisters were so confused and intermingled in his
recollection that they melted the one in the other, and became in some
measure the image of one and the same person. Any parallel became
impossible between them, thanks to this singular confusion of the two

points of comparison. Mrs. Scott and Miss Percival remained thus inseparable in the thoughts of Jean until the day when it was granted to him to see them again. The impression of that meeting was not effaced; it was always there, persistent, and very sweet, till Jean began to feel disturbed.

"Is it possible" — so ran his meditations — "is it possible that I have been guilty of the folly of falling in love madly at first sight? No; one might fall in love with a woman, but not with two women at once."

That thought reassured him. He was very young, this great fellow of four-and-twenty; never had love entered fully into his heart. Love! He knew very little about it, except from books, and he had read but few of them. But he was no angel; he could find plenty of attractions in the grisettes of Souvigny, and when they would allow him to tell them that they were charming, he was quite ready to do so, but it had never entered his head to regard as love those passing fancies, which only caused the slightest and most superficial disturbance in his heart.

Paul de Lavardens had marvelous powers of enthusiasm and idealization. His heart sheltered always two or three grandes passions, which lived there in perfect harmony. Paul had been so clever as to discover, in this little town of 15,000 souls, numbers of pretty girls, all made to be adored. He always believed himself the discoverer of America, when, in fact, he had done nothing but follow in the track of other navigators.

The world-Jean had scarcely encountered it. He had allowed himself to be dragged by Paul, a dozen times, perhaps, to soirees or balls at the great houses of the neighborhood. He had invariably returned thoroughly bored, and had concluded that these pleasures were not made for him. His tastes were simple, serious. He loved solitude, work, long walks, open space, horses, and books. He was rather savage — a son of the soil. He loved his village, and all the old friends of his childhood. A quadrille in a drawing room caused him unspeakable terror; but every year, at the festival of the patron saint of Longueval, he danced gaily with the young girls and farmers' daughters of the neighborhood.

If he had seen Mrs. Scott and Miss Percival at home in Paris, in all the splendor of their luxury, in all the perfection of their costly surroundings, he would have looked at them from afar, with curiosity, as exquisite works of art. Then he would have returned home, and would have slept, as usual, the most peaceful slumber in the world.

Yes, but it was not thus that the thing had come to pass, and hence his excitement, hence his disturbance. These two women had shown themselves before him in the midst of a circle with which he was familiar, and which had been, if only for this reason, singularly favorable to them. Simple, good, frank, cordial, such they had shown themselves the very first day, and delightfully pretty into the bargain — a fact which is never insignificant. Jean fell at once under the charm; he was there still!

At the moment when he dismounted in the barrack-yard, at nine o'clock, the old priest began his campaign joyously. Since the previous evening the Abbé's head had been on fire; Jean had not slept much, but he had not slept at all. He had risen very early, and with closed doors, alone with Pauline, he had counted and recounted his money, spreading out his one hundred Louis-d'or, gloating over them like a miser, and like a miser finding exquisite pleasure in handling his hoard. All that was his! for him! that is to say, for the poor.

"Do not be too lavish, Monsieur le Curé," said Pauline; "be economical. I think that if you distribute today one hundred francs —"

"That is not enough, Pauline. I shall only have one such day in my life, but one I will have. How much do you think I shall give today?"

"How much, Monsieur le Curé?"

"One thousand francs!"

"One thousand francs!"

"Yes. We are millionaires now; we possess all the treasures of America, and you talk about economy? Not today, at all events; indeed, I have no right to think of it."

After saying mass at nine o'clock he set out and showered gold along his way. All had a share — the poor who acknowledged their poverty and those who concealed it. Each alms was accompanied by the same little discourse:

"This comes from the new owners of the Longueval — two American ladies, Mrs. Scott and Miss Percival. Remember their names, and pray for them."

Then he made off without waiting for thanks, across the fields, through the woods, from hamlet to hamlet, from cottage to cottage — on, on, on. A sort of intoxication mounted to his brain. Everywhere were cries of joy and astonishment. All these louis-d'or fell, as if by a miracle, into the poor hands accustomed to receive little pieces of silver. The Curb was guilty of follies, actual follies. He was out of bounds; he did not recognize himself; he had lost all control over himself; he even gave to those who did not expect anything.

He met Claude Rigal, the old sergeant, who had left one of his arms at Sebastopol. He was growing grey — nay, white; for time passes, and the soldiers of the Crimea will soon be old men.

"Here!" said the Curé, "I have twenty francs for you."

"Twenty francs? But I never asked for anything; I don't want anything; I have my pension."

His pension! Seven hundred francs!

"But listen; it will be something to buy you cigars. It comes from America."

And then followed the Abbé's little speech about the masters of Longueval.

He went to a poor woman whose son had gone to Tunis.

"Well, how is your son getting on?"

"Not so bad, Monsieur le Curé; I had a letter from him yesterday. He does not complain; he is very well; only he says there are no Kroomirs. Poor boy! I have been saving for a month, and I think I shall soon be able to send him ten francs."

"You shall send him thirty francs. Take this."

"Thirty francs! Monsieur le Curé, you give me thirty francs?"

"Yes, that is for you."

"For my boy?"

"For your boy. But listen; you must know from whom it comes, and you must take care to tell your son when you write to him."

Again the little speech about the new owners of Longueval, and again the adjuration to remember them in their prayers. At six o'clock he returned home, exhausted with fatigue, but with his soul filled with joy.

"I have given away all," he cried, as soon as he saw Pauline, "all! all! all!"

He dined, and then went in the evening to perform the usual service for the month of Mary. But this time, the harmonium was silent; Miss Percival was no longer there.

The little organist of the evening before was at that moment much perplexed. On two couches in her dressing-room were spread two frocks — a white and a blue. Bettina was meditating which of these two frocks she would wear to the opera that evening. After long hesitation she fixed on the blue. At half-past nine the two sisters ascended the grand staircase at the opera-house. Just as they entered their box the curtain rose on the second scene of the second act of Aida, that containing the ballet and march.

Two young men, Roger de Puymartin and Louis de Martillet, were seated in the front of a stage-box. The young ladies of the corps de ballet had not yet appeared, and these gentlemen, having no occupation, were amusing themselves with looking about the house. The appearance of Miss Percival made a strong impression upon both.

"Ah! ah!" said Puymartin, "there she is, the little golden nugget!"

"She is perfectly dazzling this evening, this little golden nugget," continued Martillet. "Look at her, at the line of her neck, the fall of her shoulders — still a young girl, and already a woman."

"Yes, she is charming, and tolerably well off into the bargain."

"Fifteen millions of her own, and the silver mine is still productive."

"Berulle told me twenty-five millions, and he is very well up in American affairs."

"Twenty-five millions! A pretty haul for Romanelli!"

"What? Romanelli!"

"Report says that that will be a match; that it is already settled."

"A match may be arranged, but with Montessan, not with Romanelli. Ah! at last! Here is the ballet."

They ceased to talk. The ballet in Aida lasts only five minutes, and for those five minutes they had come. Consequently they must be enjoyed respectfully, religiously, for there is that peculiarity among a number of the habitués of the opera, that they chatter like magpies when they ought to be silent, to listen, and that they observe the most absolute silence when they might be allowed to speak, while looking on.

The trumpets of Aida had given their last heroic 'fanfare' in honor of Rhadames before the great sphinxes under the green foliage of the palm trees, the dancers advanced, the light trembling on their spangled robes, and took possession of the stage.

With much attention and pleasure Mrs. Scott followed the evolutions of the ballet, but Bettina had suddenly become thoughtful, on perceiving in a box, on the other side of the house, a tall, dark young man. Miss Percival talked to herself, and said:

"What shall I do? What shall I decide on? Must I marry him, that handsome, tall fellow over there, who is watching me, for it is I that he is looking at? He will come into our box directly this act is over, and then I have only to say, 'I have decided; there is my hand; I will be your wife,' and then all would be settled! I should be Princess! Princess Romanelli! Princess Bettina! Bettina Romanelli! The names go well together; they sound very pretty. Would it amuse me to be a princess? Yes — and no! Among all the young men in Paris, who, during the last year, have run after my money, this Prince Romanelli is the one who pleases me best. One of these days I must make up my mind to marry. I think he loves me. Yes, but the question is, do I love him? No, I don't think I do, and I should so much like to love — so much, so much!"

At the precise moment when these reflections were passing through Bettina's pretty head, Jean, alone in his study, seated before his desk with a great book under the shade of his lamp, looked through, and took notes of, the campaigns of Turenne. He had been directed to give a course of instruction to the non-commissioned officers of the regiment, and was prudently preparing his lesson for the next day.

But in the midst of his notes — Nordlingen, 1645; les Dunes, 1658; Mulhausen and Turckheim, 1674-1675 — he suddenly perceived (Jean did not draw very badly) a sketch, a woman's portrait, which all at once appeared under his pen. What was she doing there, in the middle of Turenne's victories, this pretty little woman? And then who was she — Mrs. Scott or Miss Percival? How could he tell? They resembled each other so much; and, laboriously, Jean returned to the history of the campaigns of Turenne.

And at the same moment, the Abbé Constantin, on his knees before his little wooden bedstead, called down, with all the strength of his soul, the blessings of Heaven on the two women through whose bounty he had passed such a sweet and happy day. He prayed God to bless Mrs. Scott in her children, and to give to Miss Percival a husband after her own heart.

Chapter V

THE FAIR AMERICANS

*F*ormerly Paris belonged to the Parisians, and that at no very remote period-thirty or forty years ago. At that epoch the French were the masters of Paris, as the English are the masters of London, the Spaniards of Madrid, and the Russians of St. Petersburg. Those times are no more. Other countries still have their frontiers; there are now none to France. Paris has become an immense Babel, a universal and international city. Foreigners do not only come to visit Paris; they come there to live. At the present day we have in Paris a Russian colony, a Spanish colony, a Levantine colony, an American colony. The foreigners have already conquered from us the greater part of the Champs-Elysées and the Boulevard Malesherbes; they advance, they extend their outworks; we retreat, pressed back by the invaders; we are obliged to expatriate ourselves. We have begun to found Parisian colonies in the plains of Passy, in the plain of Monceau, in quarters which formerly were not Paris at all, and which are not quite even now. Among the foreign colonies, the richest, the most populous, the most brilliant, is the American colony. There is a moment when an American feels himself rich enough, a Frenchman never. The American then stops, draws breath, and while still husbanding the capital, no longer spares the income. He knows how to spend, the Frenchman knows only how to save.

The Frenchman has only one real luxury — his revolutions. Prudently and wisely he reserves himself for them, knowing well that they will cost France dear, but that, at the same time, they will furnish the opportunity for advantageous investments. The Frenchman says to himself:

"Let us hoard! let us hoard! let us hoard! Some of these mornings there will be a revolution, which will make the 5 percents fall 50 or 60 francs. I will buy then. Since revolutions are inevitable, let us try at least to make them profitable."

They are always talking about the people who are ruined by revolutions, but perhaps the number of those enriched by revolutions is still greater.

The Americans experience the attraction of Paris very strongly. There is no town in the world where it is easier or more agreeable to spend a great dial of money. For many reasons, both of race and origin, this attraction exercised over Mrs. Scott and Miss Percival a very remarkable power.

The most French of our colonies is Canada, which is no longer ours. The recollection of their first home has been preserved faithfully and tenderly in the hearts of the emigrants to Montreal and Quebec. Susie Percival had received from her mother an entirely French education, and she had brought up her sister in the same love of our country. The two sisters felt themselves Frenchwomen; still better, Parisians. As soon as the avalanche of dollars had descended upon them, the same desire seized them both — to come and live in Paris. They demanded France as if it had been their fatherland. Mr. Scott made some opposition.

"If I go away from here," he said, "your incomes will suffer."

"What does that matter?" replied Susie. "We are rich — too rich. Do let us go. We shall be so happy, so delighted!"

Mr. Scott allowed himself to be persuaded, and, at the beginning of January, 1880, Susie wrote the following letter to her friend, Katie Norton, who had lived in Paris for some years:

"Victory! It is decided! Richard has consented. I shall arrive in April, and become a Frenchwoman again. You offered to undertake all the preparations for our settlement in Paris. I am horribly presuming — I accept! When I arrive in Paris, I should like to be able to enjoy Paris, and not be obliged to lose my first month in running after upholsterers, coach-builders, horse-dealers. I should like, on arriving at the railway station, to find awaiting me my carriage, my coachman, my horses. That very day I should like you to dine with me at my home. Hire or buy a mansion, engage the servants, choose the horses, the carriages, the liveries. I depend entirely upon you. As long as the liveries are blue, that is the only point. This line is added at the request of Bettina.

"We shall bring only seven persons with us. Richard will have his valet, Bettina and I two ladies' maids; then there are the two governesses for the children, and, besides these, two boys, Toby and Bobby, who ride to perfection. We should never find in Paris such a perfect pair.

"Everything else, people and things, we shall leave in New York. No, not quite everything; I had for gotten four little ponies, four little gems, black as ink. We have not the heart to leave them; we shall drive them in a phaeton; it is delightful. Both Bettina and I drive four-in-hand very well. Ladies can drive four-in-hand in the Bois very early in the morning; can't they? Here it is quite possible. Above all, my dear Katie, do not consider money. Be as extravagant as you like, that is all I ask." The same day that Mrs. Norton received this letter witnessed the failure of a certain Garneville. He was a great speculator who had been on a false scent. Stocks had fallen just when he had expected a rise. This Garneville had, six weeks before, installed himself in a brand-new house, which had no other fault than a too startling magnificence. Mrs. Norton signed an agreement — 100,000 francs a year, with the option of buying house and furniture for 2,000,000 during the first year of possession. A famous upholsterer undertook to correct and subdue the exaggerated splendor of a loud and gorgeous luxury. That done, Mrs. Scott's friend had the good fortune to lay her hand on two of those eminent artists without whom the routine of a great house can neither be established nor carried on. The first, a chef of the first rank, who had just left an ancient mansion of the Faubourg St. Germain, to his great regret, for he had aristocratic inclinations.

"Never," said he to Mrs. Norton, "never would I have left the service of Madame la Duchesse if she had kept up her establishment on the same footing as formerly; but Madame la Duchesse has four children — two sons who have run through a good deal, and two daughters who will soon be of an age to marry; they must have their dowries. Therefore, Madame la Duchesse is obliged to draw in a little, and the house is no longer important enough for me."

This distinguished character, of course, made his conditions. Though excessive, they did not alarm Mrs. Norton, who knew that he was a man of the most serious merit; but he, before deciding, asked permission to telegraph to New York. He wished to make certain inquiries. The reply was favorable; he accepted.

The second great artist was a stud-groom of the rarest and highest capacity, who was just about to retire after having made his fortune. He consented, however, to organize the stables for Mrs. Scott. It was thoroughly understood that he should have every liberty in purchasing the horses, that he should wear no livery, that he should choose the coachmen, the grooms, and everyone connected with the stables; that he should never have less than fifteen horses in the stables, that no bargain should be made with the coach-builder or saddler without his intervention, and that he should never mount the box, except early in the morning, in plain clothes, to give lessons in driving to the ladies and children, if necessary.

The cook took possession of his stores, and the stud-groom of his stables. Everything else was only a question of money, and with regard to this Mrs. Norton made full use of her extensive powers. She acted in conformity with the instructions she had received. In the short space of two months she performed prodigies, and that is how, when, on the 15th of April, 1880, Mr. Scott, Susie, and Bettina alighted from the mail train from Havre, at half-past four in the afternoon, they found Mrs. Norton at the station of St. Lazare, who said:

"Your calèche is there in the yard; behind it is a landau for the children; and behind the landau is an omnibus for the servants. The three carriages bear your monogram, are driven by your coachman, and drawn by your horses. Your address is 24 Rue Murillo, and here is the menu of your dinner tonight. You invited me two months ago; I accept, and will even take the liberty of bringing a dozen friends with me. I shall furnish everything, even the guests. But do not be alarmed; you know them all; they are mutual friends, and this evening we shall be able to judge of the merits of your cook."

The first Parisian who had the honor and pleasure of paying homage to the beauty of Mrs. Scott and Miss Percival was a little Marmiton fifteen years old, who stood there in his white clothes, his wicker basket on his head, at the moment when Mrs. Scott's carriage, entangled in the multitude of vehicles, slowly worked its way out of the station. The little cook stopped short on the pavement, opened wide his eyes, looked at the two sisters with amazement, and boldly cast full in their faces the single word:

"Mazette!"

When Madame Recamier saw her first wrinkles, and first grey hairs, she said to a friend:

"Ah! my dear, there are no more illusions left for me! From the day when I saw that the little chimney-sweeps no longer turned round in the street to look at me, I understood that all was over."

The opinion of the confectioners' boys is, in similar cases, of equal value with the opinion of the little chimney-sweeps. All was not over for Susie and Bettina; on the contrary, all was only beginning.

Five minutes later, Mrs. Scott's carriage was ascending the Boulevard Haussmann to the slow and measured trot of a pair of admirable horses. Paris counted two Parisians the more.

The success of Mrs. Scott and Miss Percival was immediate, decisive, like a flash of lightning. The beauties of Paris are not classed and catalogued like the beauties of London; they do not publish their portraits in the illustrated papers, or allow their photographs to be sold at the stationers. However, there is always a little staff, consisting of a score of women, who represent the grace, and charm, and beauty of Paris, which women, after ten or twelve years' service, pass into the reserve, just like the old generals. Susie and Bettina immediately became part of this little staff. It was an affair of four-and-twenty hours — of less than four-and-twenty hours, for all passed between eight in the morning and midnight, the day after their arrival in Paris.

Imagine a sort of little *feerie*, in three acts, of which the success increases from tableau to tableau:

1st. A ride at ten in the morning in the Bois, with the two marvelous grooms imported from America.

2d. A walk at six o'clock in the Allee des Acacias.

3d. An appearance at the opera at ten in the evening in Mrs. Norton's box.

The two novelties were immediately remarked, and appreciated as they deserved to be, by the thirty or forty persons who constitute a sort of mysterious tribunal, and who, in the name of all Paris, pass sentence beyond appeal. These thirty or forty persons have, from time to time, the fancy to declare "delicious" some woman who is manifestly ugly. That is enough; she is "delicious" from that moment.

The beauty of the two sisters was unquestionable. In the morning, it was their grace, their elegance, their distinction that attracted universal admiration; in the afternoon, it was declared that their walk had the freedom and ease of two young goddesses; in the evening, there was but one cry of rapture at the ideal perfection of their shoulders. From that moment, all Paris had for the two sisters the eyes of the little pastry-cook of the Rue d'Amsterdam; all Paris repeated his *Mazette*, though naturally with the variations and developments imposed by the usages of the world.

Mrs. Scott's drawing room immediately became the fashion. The habitués of three or four great American houses transferred themselves to the Scotts, who had three hundred persons at their first Wednesday. Their circle increased; there was a little of everything to be found in their set — Americans, Spaniards, Italians, Hungarians, Russians, and even Parisians.

When she had related her history to the Abbé Constantin, Mrs. Scott had not told all — one never does tell all. In a word, she was a coquette. Mr. Scott had the most perfect confidence in his wife, and left her entire liberty. He appeared very little; he was an honorable man, who felt a vague embarrassment at having made such a marriage, at having married so much money.

Having a taste for business, he had great pleasure in devoting himself entirely to the administering of the two immense fortunes which were in his hands, in continually increasing them, and in saying every year to his wife and sister in-law:

"You are still richer than you were last year!"

Not content with watching with much prudence and ability over the interests which he had left in America, he launched in France into large speculations, and was as successful in Paris as he had been in New York. In order to make money, the first thing is to have no need of it.

They made love to Mrs. Scott to an enormous extent; they made love to her in French, in Italian, in English, in Spanish; for she knew those four languages, and there is one advantage that foreigners have over our poor Parisians, who usually know only their mother tongue, and have not the resource of international passions.

Naturally, Mrs. Scott did not drive her adorers from her presence. She had ten, twenty, thirty at a time.

No one could boast of any preference; to all she opposed the same amiable, laughing, joyous resistance. It was clear to all that the game amused her, and that she did not for a moment take it seriously. Mr. Scott never felt a moment's anxiety, and he was perfectly right. More, he enjoyed his wife's successes; he was happy in seeing her happy. He loved her dearly — a little more than she loved him. She loved him very much, and that was all. There is a great difference between dearly and very much when these two adverbs are placed after the verb to love.

As to Bettina, around her was a maddening whirl, an orgy of adulation. Such fortune! Such beauty! Miss Percival arrived in Paris on the 15th of April; a fortnight had not passed before the offers of marriage began to pour upon her. In the course of that first year, she might, had she wished it, have been married thirty-four times, and to what a variety of suitors!

They asked her hand for a young exile, who, under certain circumstances, might be called to ascend a throne — a very small one, it is true, but a throne nevertheless.

They asked her hand for a young duke, who would make a great figure at Court when France — as was inevitable — should recognize her errors, and bow down before her legitimate masters.

They asked her hand for a young prince, who would have a place on the steps of the throne when France — as was inevitable — should again knit together the chain of the Napoleonic traditions.

They asked her hand for a young Republican deputy, who had just made a most brilliant debut in the Chamber, and for whom the future reserved the most splendid destiny, for the Republic was now established in France on the most indestructible basis.

They asked her hand for a young Spaniard of the purest lineage, and she was given to understand that the *contrat* would be signed in the palace of a queen, who does not live far from the Arc de Triomphe.

Besides, one can find her address in the *Almanach Bottin,* for at the present day, there are queens who have their address in Bottin between an attorney and a druggist; it is only the kings of France who no longer live in France.

They asked her hand for the son of a peer of England, and for the son of a member of the highest Viennese aristocracy; for the son of a Parisian banker, and for the son of a Russian ambassador; for a Hungarian count, and for an Italian prince; and also for various excellent young men who were nothing and had nothing — neither name nor fortune; but Bettina had granted them a waltz, and, believing themselves irresistible, they hoped that they had caused a flutter of that little heart.

But up to the present moment nothing had touched that little heart, and the reply had been the same to all "No! no!" again "No!" always "No!"

Some days after that performance of Aida, the two sisters had a rather long conversation on this great, this eternal question of marriage. A certain name had been pronounced by Mrs. Scott which had provoked on the part of Miss Percival the most decided and most energetic refusal, and Susie had laughingly said to her sister:

"But, Bettina, you will be obliged to end by marrying."

"Yes, certainly, but I should be so sorry to marry without love. It seems to me that before I could resolve to do such a thing I must be in danger of dying an old maid, and I am not yet that."

"No, not yet."

"Let us wait, let us wait."

"Let us wait. But among all these lovers whom you have been dragging after you for the last year, there have been some very nice, very amiable, and it is really a little strange if none of them —"

"None, my Susie, none, absolutely none. Why should I not tell you the truth? Is it their fault? Have they gone unskillfully to work? Could they, in managing better, have found the way to my heart? or is the fault in me? Is it perhaps, that the way to my heart is a steep, rocky, inaccessible way, by which no one will ever pass? Am I a horrid little creature, and, cold, and condemned never to love?"

"I do not think so."

"Neither do I, but up to the present time that is my history. No, I have never felt anything which resembled love. You are laughing, and I can guess why. You are saying to yourself, 'A little girl like that pretending to know what love is!' You are right; I do not know, but I have a pretty good idea. To love — is it not to prefer to all in the world one certain person?"

"Yes; it is really that."

"Is it not never to weary of seeing that person, or of hearing him? Is it not to cease to live when he is not there, and to immediately begin to revive when he reappears?"

"Oh, but this is romantic love."

"Well, that is the love of which I dream, and that is the love which does not come — not at all till now; and yet that person preferred by me to all and everything does exist. Do you know who it is?"

"No, I do not know; I do not know, but I have a little suspicion."

"Yes, it is you, my dearest, and it is perhaps you, naughty sister, who makes me so insensible and cruel on this point. I love you too much; you fill my heart; you have occupied it entirely; there is no room for anyone else. Prefer anyone to you! Love anyone more than you! That will never, never be!"

"Oh, yes, it will."

"Oh, no. Love differently, perhaps, but more — no. He must not count upon that, this gentleman whom I expect, and who does not arrive."

"Do not be afraid, my Betty, there is room in your heart for all whom you should love — for your husband, for your children, and that without your old sister losing anything. The heart is very little, but it is also very large."

Bettina tenderly embraced her sister; then, resting her head coaxingly on Susie's shoulder, she said:

"If, however, you are tired of keeping me with you, if you are in a hurry to get rid of me, do you know what I will do? I will put the names of two of these gentlemen in a basket, and draw lots. There are two who at the last extremity would not be absolutely disagreeable."

"Which two?"

"Guess."

"Prince Romanelli."

"For one! And the other?"

"Monsieur de Montessan."

"Those are the two! It is just that. Those two would be acceptable, but only acceptable, and that is not enough."

This is why Bettina awaited with extreme impatience the day when she should leave Paris, and take up their abode in Longueval. She was a little tired of so much pleasure, so much success, so many offers of marriage. The whirlpool of Parisian gayety had seized her on her arrival, and would not let her go, not for one hour of halt or rest. She felt the need of being given up to herself for a few days, to herself alone, to consult and question herself at her leisure, in the complete solitude of the country-in a word, to belong to herself again.

Was not Bettina all sprightly and joyous when, on the 14th of June, they took the train for Longueval? As soon as she was alone in a coupe with her sister:

"Ah!" she cried, "how happy I am! Let us breathe a little, quite alone, you and me, for a few days. The Nortons and Turners do not come till the 25th, do they?"

"No, not till the 25th."

"We will pass our lives riding or driving in the woods, in the fields. Ten days of liberty! And during those ten days no more lovers, no more lovers! And all those lovers, with what are they in love, with me or my money? That is the mystery, the unfathomable mystery."

The engine whistled; the train put itself slowly into motion. A wild idea entered Bettina's head. She leaned out of the window and cried, accompanying her words with a little wave of the hand:

"Good-bye, my lovers, good-bye."

Then she threw herself suddenly into a corner of the coupe with a hearty burst of laughter.

"Oh, Susie, Susie!"

"What is the matter?"

"A man with a red flag in his hand; he saw me, and he looked so astonished."

"You are so irrational!"

"Yes, it is true, to have called out of the window like that, but not to be happy at thinking that we are going to live alone, *en garçons.*"

"Alone! alone! Not exactly that. To begin with, we shall have two people to dinner tonight."

"Ah! that is true. But those two people, I shall not be at all sorry to see them again. Yes, I shall be well pleased to see the old Curé again, but especially the young officer."

"What! especially?"

"Certainly; because what the lawyer from Souvigny told us the other day is so touching, and what that great artilleryman did when he was quite little was so good, so good, that this evening I shall seek for an opportunity of telling him what I think of it, and I shall find one."

Then Bettina, abruptly changing the course of the conversation, continued:

"Did they send the telegram yesterday to Edwards about the ponies?"

"Yes, yesterday before dinner."

"Oh, you will let me drive them up to the house. It will be such fun to go through the town, and to drive up at full speed into the court in front of the entrance. Tell me, will you?"

"Yes, certainly, you shall drive the ponies."

"Oh, how nice of you, Susie!"

Edwards was the stud-groom. He had arrived at Longueval three days before. He deigned to come himself — to meet Mrs. Scott and Miss Percival. He brought the phaeton drawn by the four black ponies. He was waiting at the station. The passage of the ponies through the principal street of the town had made a sensation. The population rushed out of their houses, and asked eagerly:

"What is it? What can it be?"

Some ventured the opinion:

"It is, perhaps, a traveling circus."

But exclamations arose on all sides:

"You did not notice the style of it — the carriage and the harness shining like gold, and the little horses with their white rosettes on each side of the head."

The crowd collected around the station, and those who were curious learned that they were going to witness the arrival of the new owners of Longueval. They were slightly disenchanted when the two sisters appeared, very pretty, but in very simple traveling costumes.

These good people had almost expected the apparition of two princesses out of fairy tales, clad in silk and brocade, sparkling with rubies and diamonds. But they opened wide their eyes when they saw Bettina walk slowly round the four ponies, caressing one after another lightly with her hand, and examining all the details of the team with the air of a connoisseur.

Having made her inspection, Bettina, without the least hurry, drew off her long Swedish gloves, and replaced them by a pair of dog-skin which she took from the pocket of the carriage apron. Then she slipped on to the box in the place of Edwards, receiving from him the reins and whip with extreme dexterity, without allowing the already excited horses to perceive that they had changed hands.

Mrs. Scott seated herself beside her sister. The ponies pranced, curveted, and threatened to rear.

"Be very careful, miss," said Edwards; "the ponies are very fresh today."

"Do not be afraid," replied Bettina. "I know them."

Miss Percival had a hand at once very firm, very light, and very just. She held in the ponies for a few moments, forcing them to keep their own places; then, waving the long thong of her whip round the leaders, she started her little team at once, with incomparable skill, and left the station with an air of triumph, in the midst of a long murmur of astonishment and admiration.

The trot of the black ponies rang on the little oval paving-stones of Souvigny. Bettina held them well together until she had left the town, but as soon as she saw before her a clear mile and a half of highroad-almost on a dead level-she let them gradually increase their speed, till they went like the wind.

"Oh! how happy I am, Susie!" cried she; "and we shall trot and gallop all alone on these roads. Susie, would you like to drive? It is such a delight when one can let them go at full speed. They are so spirited and so gentle. Come, take the reins."

"No; keep them. It is a greater pleasure to me to see you happy."

"Oh, as to that, I am perfectly happy. I do like so much to drive four-in-hand with plenty of space before me. At Paris, even in the morning, I did not dare to any longer. They looked at me so, it annoyed me. But here — no one! no one! no one!"

At the moment when Bettina, already a little intoxicated with the bracing air and liberty, gave forth triumphantly these three exclamations, "No one! no one! no one!" a rider appeared, walking his horse in the direction of the carriage. It was Paul de Lavardens. He had been watching for more than an hour for the pleasure of seeing the Americans pass.

"You are mistaken," said Susie to Bettina; "there is someone."

"A peasant; they don't count; they won't ask me to marry them."

"It is not a peasant at all. Look!"

Paul de Lavardens, while passing the carriage, made the two sisters a highly correct bow, from which one at once scented the Parisian.

The ponies were going at such a rate that the meeting was over like a flash of lightning.

Bettina cried:

"Who is that gentleman who has just bowed to us?"

"I had scarcely time to see, but I seemed to recognize him."

"You recognized him?"

"Yes, and I would wager that I have seen him at our house this winter."

"Heavens! if it should be one of the thirty-four! Is all that going to begin again?"

Chapter VI

A LITTLE DINNER FOR FOUR

*T*hat same day, at half-past seven, Jean went to fetch the Curé, and the two walked together up to the house. During the last month a perfect army of workmen had taken possession of Longueval; all the inns in the village were making their fortunes.

Enormous furniture wagons brought cargoes of furniture and decorations from Paris. Forty-eight hours before the arrival of Mrs. Scott, Mademoiselle Marbeau, the postmistress, and Madame Lormier, the mayoress, had wormed themselves into the castle, and the account they gave of the interior turned everyone's head. The old furniture had disappeared, banished to the attics; one moved among a perfect accumulation of wonders. And the stables! and the coach-houses! A special train had brought from Paris, under the high superintendence of Edwards, a dozen carriages — and such carriages! Twenty horses — and such horses!

The Abbé Constantin thought that he knew what luxury was. Once a year he dined with his bishop, Monseigneur Faubert, a rich and amiable prelate, who entertained rather largely. The Curé, till now, had thought that there was nothing in the world more sumptuous than the Episcopal palace of Souvigny, or the castles of Lavardens and Longueval.

He began to understand, from what he was told of the new splendors of Longueval, that the luxury of the great houses of the present day must surpass to a singular degree the sober and severe luxury of the great houses of former times.

As soon as the Curé and Jean had entered the avenue in the park, which led to the house:

"Look! Jean," said the Curé; "what a change! All this part of the park used to be quite neglected, and now all the paths are graveled and raked. I shall not be able to feel myself at home as I used to do: it will be too grand. I shall not find again my old brown velvet easy chair, in which

I so often fell asleep after dinner, and if I fall asleep this evening what will become of me? You will think of it, Jean, and if you see that I begin to forget myself, you will come behind me and pinch my arm gently, won't you? You promise me?"

"Certainly, certainly, I promise you."

Jean paid but slight attention to the conversation of the Curé. He felt extremely impatient to see Mrs. Scott and Miss Percival again, but this impatience was mingled with very keen anxiety. Would he find them in the great salon at Longueval the same as he had seen them in the little dining room at the vicarage? Perhaps, instead of those two women, so perfectly simple and familiar, amusing themselves with this little improvised dinner, and who, the very first day, had treated him with so much grace and cordiality, would he find two pretty dolls-worldly, elegant, cold, and correct? Would his first impression be effaced? Would it disappear? or, on the contrary, would the impression in his heart become still sweeter and deeper?

They ascended the six steps at the entrance, and were received in the hall by two tall footmen with the most dignified and imposing air. This hall had formerly been a vast, frigid apartment, with bare stone walls. These walls were now covered with admirable tapestry, representing mythological subjects. The Curé dared scarcely glance at this tapestry; it was enough for him to perceive that the goddesses who wandered through these shades wore costumes of antique simplicity.

One of the footmen opened wide the folding-doors of the salon. It was there that one had generally found the old Marquise, on the right of the high chimneypiece, and on the left had stood the brown velvet easy chair.

No brown easy chair now! That old relic of the Empire, which was the basis of the arrangement of the salon, had been replaced by a marvelous specimen of tapestry of the end of the last century. Then a crowd of little easy chairs, and ottomans of all forms and all colors, were scattered here and there with an appearance of disorder which was the perfection of art.

As soon as Mrs. Scott saw the Curé and Jean enter, she rose, and going to meet them, said:

"How kind of you to come, Monsieur le Curé, and you, too, Monsieur Jean. How pleased I am to see you, my first, my only friends down here!"

Jean breathed again. It was the same woman.

"Will you allow me," added Mrs. Scott, "to introduce my children to you? Harry and Bella, come here."

Harry was a very pretty little boy of six, and Bella a very charming little girl, five years old. They had their mother's large, dark eyes, and her golden hair.

After the Curé had kissed the two children, Harry, who was looking with admiration at Jean's uniform, said to his mother:

"And the soldier, mamma, must we kiss him, too?"

"If you like," replied Mrs. Scott, "and if he will allow it."

A moment after, the two children were installed upon Jean's knees, and overwhelming him with questions.

"Are you an officer?"

"Yes, I am an officer."

"What in?"

"In the artillery."

"The artillery! Oh, you are one of the men who fire the cannon. Oh, how I should like to be quite near when they fire the cannon!"

"Will you take us some day when they fire the cannon? Tell me, will you?"

Meanwhile, Mrs. Scott chatted with the Curé, and Jean, while replying to the children's questions, looked at Mrs. Scott. She wore a white muslin frock, but the muslin disappeared under a complete avalanche of little flounces of Valenciennes. The dress was cut out in front in a large square, her arms were bare to the elbow, a large bouquet of red roses at the opening of her dress, a red rose fixed in her hair, with a diamond *agraffe* — nothing more.

Mrs. Scott suddenly perceived that the children had taken entire possession of Jean, and exclaimed:

"Oh, I beg your pardon. Harry, Bella!"

"Oh, pray let them stay with me."

"I am so sorry to keep you waiting for dinner; my sister is not down yet. Oh! here she is!"

Bettina entered. The same frock of white muslin, the same delicate mass of lace, the same red roses, the same grace, the same beauty, and the same smiling, amiable, candid manner.

"How do you do, Monsieur le Curé? I am delighted to see you. Have you pardoned my dreadful intrusion of the other day?"

Then, turning toward Jean and offering him her hand:

"How do you do, Monsieur — Monsieur — Oh! I can not remember your name, and yet we seem to be already old friends, Monsieur —"

"Jean Reynaud."

"Jean Reynaud, that is it. How do you do, Monsieur Reynaud? I warn you faithfully that when we really are old friends — that is to say, in about a week — I shall call you Monsieur Jean. It is a pretty name, Jean."

Up to the moment when Bettina appeared Jean had said to himself: "Mrs. Scott is the prettier!"

When he felt Bettina's little hand slip into his arm, and when she turned toward him her delicious face, he said:

"Miss Percival is the prettier!"

But his perplexities gathered round him again when he was seated between the two sisters. If he looked to the right, love threatened him from that direction, and if he looked to the left, the danger removed immediately, and passed to the left.

Conversation began, easy, animated, confidential. The two sisters were charmed; they had already walked in the park; they promised themselves a long ride in the forest tomorrow. Riding was their passion, their madness. It was also Jean's passion, so that after a quarter of an hour they begged him to join them the next day. There was no one who knew the country round better than he did; it was his native place. He should be so happy to do the honors of it, and to show them numbers of delightful little spots which, without him, they would never discover.

"Do you ride every day?" asked Bettina.

"Every day and sometimes twice. In the morning on duty, and in the evening I am ride for my own pleasure."

"Early in the morning?"

"At half-past five."

"At half-past five every morning?"

"Yes, except Sunday."

"Then you get up —"

"At half-past four."

"And is it light?"

"Oh, just now, broad daylight."

"To get up at half-past four is admirable; we often finish our day just when yours is beginning. And are you fond of your profession?"

"Very. It is an excellent thing to have one's life plain before one, with exact and definite duties."

"And yet," said Mrs. Scott, "not to be one's own master — to be always obliged to obey."

"That is perhaps what suits me best; there is nothing easier than to obey, and then to learn to obey is the only way of learning to command."

"Ah! since you say so, it must be true."

"Yes, no doubt," added the Curé; "but he does not tell you that he is the most distinguished officer in his regiment, that —"

"Oh! pray do not."

The Curé, in spite of the resistance of Jean, was about to launch into a panegyric on his godson, when Bettina, interposing, said:

"It is unnecessary, Monsieur le Curé, do not say anything, we know already all that you would tell us, we have been so indiscreet as to make inquiries about Monsieur — oh, I was just going to say Monsieur Jean — about Monsieur Reynaud. Well, the information we received was excellent!"

"I am curious to know," said Jean.

"Nothing! nothing! you shall know nothing. I do not wish to make you blush, and you would be obliged to blush."

Then turning toward the Curé, "And about you, too, Monsieur l'Abbé, we have had some information. It appears that you are a saint."

"Oh! as to that, it is perfectly true," cried Jean.

It was the Curé this time who cut short the eloquence of Jean. Dinner was almost over. The old priest had not got through this dinner without experiencing many emotions. They had repeatedly presented to him complicated and scientific constructions upon which he had only ventured with a trembling hand. He was afraid of seeing the whole crumble beneath his touch; the trembling castles of jelly, the pyramids of truffles, the fortresses of cream, the bastions of pastry, the rocks of ice. Otherwise the Abbé Constantin dined with an excellent appetite, and did not recoil before two or three glasses of champagne. He was no foe to good cheer; perfection is not of this world; and if gormandizing were, as they say, a cardinal sin, how many good priests would be damned!

Coffee was served on the terrace in front of the house; in the distance was heard the harsh voice of the old village clock striking nine. Woods and fields were slumbering; the avenues in the park showed only as long, undulating, and undecided lines. The moon slowly rose over the tops of the great trees.

Bettina took a box of cigars from the table. "Do you smoke?" said she.

"Yes, Miss Percival."

"Take one, Monsieur Jean. It can't be helped. I have said it. Take one — but no, listen to me first."

And speaking in a low voice, while offering him the box of cigars:

"It is getting dark, now you may blush at your ease. I will tell you what I did not say at dinner. An old lawyer in Souvigny, who was your guardian, came to see my sister in Paris, about the payment for the place; he told us what you did after your father's death, when you were only a child, what you did for that poor mother, and for that poor young girl. Both my sister and I were much touched by it."

"Yes," continued Mrs. Scott, "and that is why we have received you today with so much pleasure. We should not have given such a reception to everyone, of that you may be sure. Well, now take your cigar, my sister is waiting."

Jean could not find a word in reply. Bettina stood there with the box of cigars in her two hands, her eyes fixed frankly on the countenance of Jean. At the moment, she tasted a true and keen pleasure which may be expressed by this phrase:

"It seems to me that I see before me a man of honor."

"And now," said Mrs. Scott, "let us sit here and enjoy this delicious night; take your coffee, smoke —"

"And do not let us talk, Susie, do not let us talk. This great silence of the country, after the great noise and bustle of Paris, is delightful! Let us sit here without speaking; let us look at the sky, the moon, and the stars."

All four, with much pleasure, carried out this little program. Susie and Bettina, calm, reposeful, absolutely separated from their existence of yesterday, already felt a tenderness for the place which had just received them, and was going to keep them. Jean was less tranquil; the words of Miss Percival had caused him profound emotion, his heart had not yet quite regained its regular throb.

But the happiest of all was the Abbé Constantin.

This little episode which had caused Jean's modesty such a rude, yet sweet trial, had brought him exquisite joy, the Abbé bore his godson such affection. The most tender father never loved more warmly the dearest of his children. When the old Curé looked at the young officer, he often said to himself:

"Heaven has been too kind; I am a priest, and I have a son!"

The Abbé sank into a very agreeable reverie; he felt himself at home, he felt himself too much at home; by degrees his ideas became hazy and confused, reverie became drowsiness, drowsiness became slumber, the disaster was soon complete, irreparable; the Curé slept, and slept profoundly. This marvelous dinner, and the two or three glasses of champagne may have had something to do with the catastrophe.

Jean perceived nothing; he had forgotten the promise made to his godfather. And why had he forgotten it? Because Mrs. Scott and Miss Percival had thought proper to put their feet on the footstools, placed in front of their great wicker garden-chairs filled with cushions; then they had thrown themselves lazily back in their chairs, and their muslin skirts had become raised a little, a very little, but yet enough to display four little feet, the lines of which showed very distinctly and clearly beneath two pretty clouds of white lace. Jean looked at these little feet, and asked himself this question:

"Which are the smaller?"

While he was trying to solve this problem, Bettina, all at once, said to him in a low voice:

"Monsieur Jean! Monsieur Jean!"

"Miss Percival?"

"Look at the Curé, he is asleep."

"Oh! it is my fault."

"How your fault?" asked Mrs. Scott, also in a low voice.

"Yes; my godfather rises at daybreak, and goes to bed very early; he told me to be sure and prevent his falling asleep; when Madame de Longueval was here he very often had a nap after dinner. You have shown him so much kindness that he has fallen back into his old habits."

"And he is perfectly right," said Bettina, "do not make a noise, do not wake him."

"You are too good, Miss Percival, but the air is getting a little fresh."

"Ah! that is true, he might catch cold. Stay, I will go and fetch a wrap for him."

"I think, Miss Percival, it would be better to try and wake him skillfully, so that he should not suspect that you had seen him asleep."

"Let me do it," said Bettina. "Susie, let us sing together, very softly at first, then we will raise our voices little by little, let us sing."

"Willingly, but what shall we sing?"

"Let us sing, *Quelque chose d'enfantin,* the words are suitable."

Susie and Bettina began to sing:

If I had but two little wings,
And were a little feathery bird,

Their sweet and penetrating voices had an exquisite sonority in that profound silence. The Abbé heard nothing, did not move. Charmed with this little concert, Jean said to himself:

"Heaven grant that my godfather may not wake too soon!"

The voices became clearer and louder:

But in my sleep to you I fly,
I'm always with you in my sleep.

Yet the Abbé did not stir.

"How he sleeps," said Susie, "it is a crime to wake him."

"But we must; louder, Susie, louder."

Susie and Bettina both gave free scope to the power of their voices.

Sleep stays not, though a monarch bids,

So I love to wake ere break of day.

The Curé woke with a start. After a short moment of anxiety he breathed again. Evidently no one had noticed that he had been asleep. He collected himself, stretched himself prudently, slowly, he was saved!

A quarter of an hour later the two sisters accompanied the Curé and Jean to the little gate of the park, which opened into the village a few yards from the vicarage; they had nearly reached the gate when Bettina said all at once to Jean:

"Ah! all this time I have had a question to ask you. This morning when we arrived, we met on the way a slight young man, with a fair mustache, he was riding a black horse, and bowed to us as we passed."

"It was Paul de Lavardens, one of my friends; he has already had the honor of being introduced to you, but rather vaguely, and his ambition is to be presented again."

"Well, you shall bring him one of these days," said Mrs. Scott.

"After the 25th!" cried Bettina. "Not before! not before! No one till then; till then we will see no one but you, Monsieur Jean. But you, it is very extraordinary, and I don't quite know how it has happened, you don't seem anybody to us. The compliment is perhaps not very well turned, but do not make a mistake, it is a compliment. I intended to be excessively amiable in speaking to you thus."

"And so you are, Miss Percival."

"So much the better if I have been so fortunate as to make myself understood. Good-bye, Monsieur Jean — till tomorrow!"

Mrs. Scott and Miss Percival returned slowly toward the castle.

"And now, Susie," said Bettina, "scold me well, I expect it, I have deserved it."

"Scold you! Why?"

"You are going to say, I am sure, that I have been too familiar with that young man."

"No, I shall not say that. From the first day that young man has made the most favorable impression upon me; he inspires me with perfect confidence."

"And so he does me."

"I am persuaded that it would be well for us both to try to make a friend of him."

"With all my heart, as far as I am concerned, so much the more as I have seen many young men since we have lived in France. Oh! yes, I have, indeed! Well! this is the first, positively the first, in whose eyes I have not clearly read, 'Oh, how glad I should be to marry the millions of that little person!' That was written in the eyes of all the others, but

not in his eyes. Now, here we are at home again. Good-night, Susie —
tomorrow."

Mrs. Scott went to see and kiss her sleeping children.

Bettina remained long, leaning on the balustrade of her balcony.

"It seems to me," said she, "that I am going to be very fond of this
place."

Chapter VII

CONFIDENCES

*T*he next morning, on returning from drill, Jean found Paul de Lavardens waiting for him at the barracks; he scarcely allowed him time to dismount, and the moment he had him alone:

"Quick," said he, "describe your, dinner-party of yesterday. I saw them myself in the morning; the little one was driving four ponies, and with an amount of audacity! I bowed to them; did they mention me? Did they recognize me? When will you take me to Longueval? Answer me."

"Answer? Yes. But which question first?"

"The last."

"When shall I take you to Longueval?"

"Yes."

"Well, in ten days; they don't want to see anyone just now."

"Then you are not going back to Longueval for ten days?"

"Oh, I shall go back today at four o'clock. But I don't count, you know. Jean Reynaud, the Curé's godson. That is why I have penetrated so easily into the confidence of these two charming women. I have presented myself under the patronage and with the guarantee of the Church. And then they have discovered that I could render them little services. I know the country very well, and they will make use of me as a guide. In a word, I am nobody; while you, Count Paul de Lavardens, you are somebody; so fear nothing, your turn will come with the fetes and balls. Then you will be resplendent in all your glory, and I shall return very humbly into my obscurity."

"You may laugh at me as much as you like; it is nonetheless true that during those ten days you will steal a march upon me — upon me!"

"How upon you?"

"Now, Jean, do you want to make me believe that you are not already in love with one of these two women? Is it possible? So much beauty, so much luxury. Luxury to that degree upsets me. Those black ponies

with their white rosettes! I dreamed of them last night, and that little-
Bettina, is it not?"

"Yes, Bettina."

"Bettina — Countess Bettina de Lavardens! Doesn't that sound well
enough! and what a perfect husband she would have in me! To be the
husband of a woman possessing boundless wealth, that is my destiny.
It is not so easy as one may suppose. I have already run through
something, and — if my mother had not stopped me! but I am quite
ready to begin again. Oh, how happy that girl would be with me! I would
create around her the existence of a fairy queen. In all her luxury she
would feel the taste, the art, and the skill of her husband. I would pass
my life in adoring her, in displaying her beauty, in petting her, in bearing
her triumphant through the world. I would study her beauty in order
to give it the frame that best suited it. 'If he were not there,' she would
say, 'I should not be so beautiful, so dazzling.' I should know not only
how to love her, but how to amuse her. She would have something for
her money, she would have love and pleasure. Come, Jean, do a good
action, take me to Mrs. Scott's today."

"I cannot, I assure you."

"Well, then, in ten days; but I give you fair notice, I shall install myself
at Longueval, and shall not move. In the first place it would please my
mother; she is still a little prejudiced against the Americans. She says
that she shall arrange not to see them, but I know my mother. Some
day, when I shall go home in the evening and tell her: 'Mother, I have
won the-heart of a charming little person who is burdened with a capital
of twenty millions — they exaggerate when they talk of hundreds of
millions. You know these are the correct figures, and they are enough
for me. That evening, then, my mother will be delighted, because, in
her heart, what is it she desires for me? What all good mothers desire
for their sons — a good marriage, or a discreet liaison with someone in
society. At Longueval I find these two essentials, and I will accommodate
myself very willingly to either. You will have the kindness to warn me
in ten days — you will let me know which of the two you abandon to
me, Mrs. Scott or Miss Percival?"

"You are mad, you are quite mad! I do not, I never shall think —"

"Listen, Jean. You are wisdom personified; you may say and do as you
like, but remember what I say to you, Jean, you will fall in love in that
house."

"I do not believe it," replied Jean, laughing.

"But I am absolutely sure of it. Good-bye. I leave you to your duties."

That morning Jean was perfectly sincere. He had slept very well the
previous night; the second interview with the two sisters had, as if by

enchantment, dissipated the slight trouble which had agitated his soul after the first meeting. He prepared to meet them again with much pleasure, but also with much tranquility; there was too much money in that house to permit the love of a poor devil like Jean to find place honestly there.

Friendship was another affair; with all his heart he wished, and with all his strength he sought, to establish himself peacefully in the esteem and regard of the sisters. He would try not to remark too much the beauty of Susie and Bettina; he would try not to forget himself as he had done the previous evening, in the contemplation of the four little feet resting on their footstools. They had said, very frankly, very cordially, to him: "You shall be our friend." That was all he desired — to be their friend — and that he would be.

During the ten days that followed, all conduced to the success of this enterprise. Susie, Bettina, the Curé, and Jean led the same life in the closest and most cordial intimacy.

Jean did not seek to analyze his feelings. He felt for these two women an equal affection; he was perfectly happy, perfectly tranquil. Then he was not in love, for love and tranquility seldom dwell at peace in the same heart.

Jean, however, saw approach, with a little anxiety and sadness, the day which would bring to Longueval the Turners, and the Nortons, and the whole force of the American colony. The day came too soon.

On Friday, the 24th of June, at four o'clock, Jean arrived at the castle. Bettina received him alone, looking quite vexed.

"How annoying it is," said she, "my sister is not well; a little headache, nothing of consequence, it will be gone by tomorrow; but I dare not ride with you alone. In America I might; but here, it would not do, would it?"

"Certainly not," replied Jean.

"I must send you back, and I am so sorry."

"And so am I — I am very sorry to be obliged to go, and to lose this last day, which I had hoped to pass with you. However, since it must be, I will come tomorrow to inquire after your sister."

"She will see you herself, tomorrow; I repeat it is nothing serious. But do not run away in such a hurry, pray; will you not spare me a little quarter of an hour's conversation? I want to speak to you; sit down there, and now listen to me well. My sister and I had intended this evening, after dinner, to blockade you into a little corner of the drawing room, and then she meant to tell you what I am going to try to say for us both."

"But I am a little nervous. Do not laugh; it is a very serious matter. We wish to thank you for having been, ever since our arrival here, so good to us both."

"Oh, Miss Percival, pray, it is I who —"

"Oh, do not interrupt me, you will quite confuse me. I do not know how to get through with it. I maintain, besides, that the thanks are due from us, not from you. We arrived here two strangers. We have been fortunate enough immediately to find friends. Yes, friends. You have taken us by the hand, you have led us to our farmers, to our keepers; while your godfather took us to his poor — and everywhere you were so much beloved that from their confidence in you, they began, on your recommendation, to like us a little. You are adored about here; do you know that?"

"I was born here — all these good people have known me from my infancy, and are grateful to me for what my grandfather and father did for them; and then I am of their race, the race of the peasants; my great-grandfather was a laborer at Bargecourt, a village two miles from here."

"Oh! oh! you appear very proud of that!"

"Neither proud nor ashamed."

"I beg your pardon, you made a little movement of pride. Well, I can tell you that my mother's great-grandfather was a farmer in Brittany. He went to Canada at the end of the last century, when Canada was still French. And you love very much this place where you were born?"

"Very much. Perhaps I shall soon be obliged to leave it."

"Why?"

"When I get promotion, I shall have to exchange into another regiment, and I shall wander from garrison to garrison; but certainly, when I am an old commandant or old colonel, on half-pay, I shall come back, and live and die here, in the little house that was my father's."

"Always quite alone?"

"Why quite alone? I certainly hope not."

"You intend to marry?"

"Yes, certainly."

"You are trying to marry?"

"No; one may think of marrying, but one ought not to try to marry."

"And yet there are people who do try. Come, I can answer for that, and you even; people have wished to marry you."

"How do you know that?"

"Oh! I know all your little affairs so well; you are what they call a good match, and I repeat it, they have wished to marry you."

"Who told you that?"

"Monsieur le Curé."

"Then he was very wrong," said Jean, with a certain sharpness.

"No, no, he was not wrong. If anyone has been to blame it is I. I soon discovered that your godfather was never so happy as when he was speaking of you. So when I was alone with him during our walks, to please him I talked of you, and he related your history to me. You are well off; you are very well off; from Government you receive every month two hundred and thirteen francs and some centimes; am I correct?"

"Yes," said Jean, deciding to bear with a good grace his share in the Curé's indiscretions.

"You have eight thousand francs' income?"

"Nearly, not quite."

"Add to that your house, which is worth thirty thousand francs. You are in an excellent position, and people have asked your hand."

"Asked my hand! No, no."

"They have, they have, twice, and you have refused two very good marriages, two very good fortunes, if you prefer it — it is the same thing for so many people. Two hundred thousand francs in the one, three hundred thousand in the other case. It appears that these fortunes are enormous for the country! Yet you have refused! Tell me why."

"Well, it concerned two charming young girls."

"That is understood. One always says that."

"But whom I scarcely knew. They forced me — for I did resist — they forced me to spend two or three evenings with them last winter."

"And then?"

"Then — I don't quite know how to explain it to you. I did not feel the slightest touch of embarrassment, emotion, anxiety, or disturbance —"

"In fact," said Bettina, resolutely, "not the least suspicion of love."

"No, not the least, and I returned quite calmly to my bachelor den, for I think it is better not to marry than to marry without love."

"And I think so, too."

She looked at him, he looked at her, and suddenly, to the great surprise of both, they found nothing more to say, nothing at all.

At this moment Harry and Bella rushed into the room, with cries of joy.

"Monsieur Jean! Are you there? Come and see our ponies!"

"Ah!" said Bettina, her voice a little uncertain, "Edwards has just come back from Paris, and has brought two microscopic ponies for the children. Let us go to see them, shall we?"

They went to see the ponies, which were indeed worthy to figure in the stables of the King of Lilliput.

Chapter VIII

ANOTHER MARTYR TO MILLIONS

*T*hree weeks have glided by; another day and Jean will be obliged to leave with his regiment for the artillery practice. He will lead the life of a soldier. Ten days' march on the highroad going and returning, and ten days in the camp at Cercottes in the forest of Orleans. The regiment will return to Souvigny on the 10th of August.

Jean is no longer tranquil; Jean is no longer happy. He sees approach with impatience, and at the same time with terror, the moment of his departure. With impatience — for he suffers an absolute martyrdom, he longs to escape from it; with terror — for to pass twenty days without seeing her, without speaking to her, without her in a word — what will become of him? Her! It is Bettina; he adores her!

Since when? Since the first day, since that meeting in the month of May in the Curé's garden. That is the truth; but Jean struggles against and resists that truth. He believes that he has only loved Bettina since the day when the two chatted gaily, amicably, in the little drawing room. She was sitting on the blue couch near the widow, and, while talking, amused herself with repairing the disorder of the dress of a Japanese princess, one of Bella's dolls, which she had left on a chair, and which Bettina had mechanically taken up.

Why had the fancy come to Miss Percival to talk to him of those two young girls whom he might have married? The question of itself was not at all embarrassing to him. He had replied that, if he had not then felt any taste for marriage, it was because his interviews with these two girls had not caused him any emotion or any agitation. He had smiled in speaking thus, but a few minutes after he smiled no more. This emotion, this agitation, he had suddenly learned to know them. Jean did not deceive himself; he acknowledged the depth of the wound; it had penetrated to his very heart's core.

Jean, however, did not abandon himself to this emotion. He said to himself:

"Yes, it is serious, very serious, but I shall recover from it."

He sought an excuse for his madness; he laid the blame on circumstances. For ten days this delightful girl had been too much with him, too much with him alone! How could he resist such a temptation? He was intoxicated with her charm, with her grace and beauty. But the next day a troop of visitors would arrive at Longueval, and there would be an end of this dangerous intimacy. He would have courage; he would keep at a distance; he would lose himself in the crowd, would see Bettina less often and less familiarly. To see her no more was a thought he could not support! He wished to remain Bettina's friend, since he could be nothing but her friend; for there was another thought which scarcely entered the mind of Jean. This thought did not appear extravagant to him; it appeared monstrous. In the whole world there was not a more honorable man than Jean, and he felt for Bettina's money horror, positively horror.

From the 25th of June the crowd had been in possession of Longueval. Mrs. Norton arrived with her son, Daniel Norton; and Mrs. Turner with her son, Philip Turner. Both of them, the young Philip and the young Daniel, formed a part of the famous brotherhood of the thirty-four. They were old friends, Bettina had treated them as such, and had declared to them, with perfect frankness, that they were losing their time. However, they were not discouraged, and formed the center of a little court which was always very eager and assiduous around Bettina.

Paul de Lavardens had made his appearance on this scene, and had very rapidly become everybody's friend. He had received the brilliant and complicated education of a young man destined for pleasure. As soon as it was a question only of amusement, riding, croquet, lawn-tennis, polo, dancing, charades, and theatricals, he was ready for everything. He excelled in everything. His superiority was evident, unquestionable. Paul became, in a short time, by general consent, the director and organizer of the fetes at Longueval.

Bettina had not a moment of hesitation. Jean introduced Paul de Lavardens, and the latter had scarcely concluded the customary little compliment when Miss Percival, leaning toward her sister, whispered in her ear:

"The thirty-fifth!"

However, she received Paul very kindly, so kindly that for several days he had the weakness to misunderstand her. He believed that it was his personal graces which had obtained for him this very flattering and cordial reception. It was a great mistake. Paul de Lavardens had been introduced by Jean; he was the friend of Jean. In Bettina's eyes, therein lay all his merit.

Mrs. Scott's castle was open house; people were not invited for one evening only, but for every evening, and Paul, with enthusiasm, came every evening! His dream was at last realized; he had, found Paris at Longueval.

But Paul was neither blind nor a fool. No doubt he was, on Miss Percival's part, the object of very particular attention and favor. It pleased her to talk long, very long, alone with him. But what was the eternal, the inexhaustible subject of their conversations? Jean, again Jean, and always Jean!

Paul was thoughtless, dissipated, frivolous, but he became in earnest when Jean was in question; he knew how to appreciate him, he knew how to love him. Nothing to him was sweeter, nothing was easier, than to say of the friend of his childhood all the good that he thought of him, and as he saw that Bettina listened with great pleasure, Paul gave free rein to his eloquence.

Only — and he was quite right — Paul wished one evening to reap the benefit of his chivalrous conduct. He had just been talking for a quarter of an hour with Bettina. The conversation finished, he went to look for Jean at the other end of the drawing room, and said to him:

"You left the field open to me, and I have made a bold stroke for Miss Percival."

"Well, you have no reason to be discontented with the result of the enterprise. You are the best friends in the world."

"Yes, certainly, pretty well, but not quite satisfactory. There is nothing more amiable or more charming than Miss Percival, and really it is very good of me to acknowledge it; for, between ourselves, she makes me play an ungrateful and ridiculous role, a role which is quite unsuited to my age. I am, you will admit, of the lover's age, and not of that of the confidant."

"Of the confidant!"

"Yes, my dear fellow, of the confidant! That is my occupation in this house. You were looking at us just now. Oh, I have very good eyes; you were looking at us. Well, do you know what we were talking about? Of you, my dear fellow, of you, of you again, of nothing but you. And it is the same thing every evening; there is no end to the questions:

"'You were brought up together? You took lessons together from the Abbé Constantin?'

"'Will he soon be Captain? And then?'

"'Commandant.'

"'And then?'

"'Colonel, etc., etc., etc.'

"Ah! I can tell you, my friend Jean, if you liked, you might dream a very delicious dream."

Jean was annoyed, almost angry. Paul was much astonished at this sudden attack of irritability.

"What is the matter? Have I said anything —"

"I beg your pardon; I was wrong. But how could you take such an absurd idea into your head?"

"Absurd! I don't see it. I have entertained the absurd idea on my own account."

"Ah! you —"

"Why 'Ah! you?' If I have had it you may have it; you are better worth it than I am."

"Paul, I entreat you!"

Jean's discomfort was evident.

"We will not speak of it again; we will not speak of it again. What I wanted to say, in short, is that Miss Percival perhaps thinks I am agreeable; but as to considering me seriously, that little person will never commit such a folly. I must fall back upon Mrs. Scott, but without much confidence. You see, Jean, I shall amuse myself in this house, but I shall make nothing out of it."

Paul de Lavardens did fall back upon Mrs. Scott, but the next day was surprised to stumble upon Jean, who had taken to placing himself very regularly in Mrs. Scott's particular circle, for like Bettina she had also her little court. But what Jean sought there was a protection, a shelter, a refuge.

The day of that memorable conversation on marriage without love, Bettina had also, for the first time, felt suddenly awake in her that necessity of loving which sleeps, but not very profoundly, in the hearts of all young girls. The sensation had been the same, at the same moment, in the soul of Bettina and the soul of Jean. He, terrified, had cast it violently from him. She, on the contrary, had yielded, in all the simplicity of her perfect innocence, to this flood of emotion and of tenderness.

She had waited for love. Could this be love? The man who was to be her thought, her life, her soul — could this be he — this Jean? Why not? She knew him better than she knew all those who, during the past year, had haunted her for her fortune, and in what she knew of him there was nothing to discourage the love of a good girl. Far from it!

Both of them did well; both of them were in the way of duty and of truth — she, in yielding; he, in resisting; she, in not thinking for a moment of the obscurity of Jean; he, in recoiling before her mountain of wealth as he would have recoiled before a crime; she, in thinking that she had no right to parley with love; he, in thinking he had no right to parley with honor.

This is why, in proportion as Bettina showed herself more tender, and abandoned herself with more frankness to the first call of love — this is why Jean became, day by day, more gloomy and more restless. He was not only afraid of loving; he was afraid of being loved.

He ought to have remained away; he should not have come near her. He had tried; he could not; the temptation was too strong; it carried him away; so he came. She would come to him, her hands extended, a smile on her lips, and her heart in her eyes. Everything in her said:

"Let us try to love each other, and if we can love, we will!"

Fear seized him. Those two hands which offered themselves to the pressure of his hands, he hardly dared touch them. He tried to escape those eyes which, tender and smiling, anxious and curious, tried to meet his eyes. He trembled before the necessity of speaking to Bettina, before the necessity of listening to her.

It was then that Jean took refuge with Mrs. Scott, and it was then that Mrs. Scott gathered those uncertain, agitated, troubled words which were not addressed to her, and which she took for herself, nevertheless. It would have been difficult not to be mistaken.

For of these still vague and confused sentiments which agitated her, Bettina had as yet said nothing. She guarded and caressed the secret of her budding love, as a miser guards and caresses the first coins of his treasure. The day when she should see clearly into her own heart; the day that she should be sure that she loved — ah! she would speak that day, and how happy she should be to tell all to Susie!

Mrs. Scott had ended by attributing to herself this melancholy of Jean, which, day by day, took a more marked character. She was flattered by it — a woman is never displeased at thinking herself beloved — and vexed at the same time. She held Jean in great esteem, in great affection; but she was greatly distressed at the thought that if he were sad and unhappy, it was because of her.

Susie was, besides, conscious of her own innocence. With others she had sometimes been coquettish, very coquettish. To torment them a little, was that such a great crime? They had nothing to do, they were good-for-nothing, it occupied them while it amused her. It helped them to pass their time, and it helped her, too. But Susie had not to reproach herself for having flirted with Jean. She recognized his merit and his superiority; he was worth more than the others, he was a man to suffer seriously, and that was what Mrs. Scott did not wish. Already, two or three times, she had been on the point of speaking to him very seriously, very affectionately, but she had reflected Jean was going away for three weeks; on his return, if it were still necessary, she would read him a lecture, and would act in such a manner that love should not come and foolishly interfere in their friendship.

So Jean was to go the next day. Bettina had insisted that he should spend this last day at Longueval, and dine at the house. Jean had refused, alleging that he had much to do the night before his departure.

He arrived in the evening, about half-past ten; he came on foot. Several times on the way he had been inclined to return.

"If I had courage enough," he said to himself, "I would not see her again. I shall leave tomorrow, and return no more to Souvigny while she is there. My resolution is taken, and taken forever."

But he continued his way, he would see her again — for the last time.

As soon as he entered the drawing room, Bettina hastened to him.

"It is you at last! How late you are!"

"I have been very busy."

"And you are going tomorrow?"

"Yes, tomorrow."

"Early?"

"At five in the morning."

"You will go by the road which runs by the wall of the park, and goes through the village?"

"Yes, that is the way we shall go."

"Why so early in the morning? I would have gone out on the terrace to see you pass, and to wish you good-bye."

Bettina detained for a moment Jean's burning hand in hers. He drew it mournfully away, with an effort.

"I must go and speak to your sister," said he.

"Directly, she has not seen you, there are a dozen persons round her. Come and sit here a little while, near me."

He was obliged to seat himself beside her.

"We are going away, too," said she.

"You!"

"Yes. An hour ago, we received a telegram from my brother-in-law, which has caused us great joy. We did not expect him for a month, but he is coming back in a fortnight. He will embark the day after tomorrow at New York, on board the Labrador. We are going to meet him at Havre. We shall also start the day after tomorrow; we are going to take the children, it will do them a great deal of good to spend a few days at the seaside. How pleased my brother-in-law will be to know you — he knows you already, we have spoken of you in all our letters. I am sure you and

Mr. Scott will get on extremely well together, he is so good. How long shall you stay away?"

"Three weeks."

"Three weeks in a camp?"

"Yes, Miss Percival, in the camp of Cercottes."

"In the middle of the forest of Orleans. I made your godfather explain all about it to me this morning. Of course I am delighted to go to meet my brother-in-law; but at the same time, I am a little sorry to leave here, for I should have gone every morning to pay a little visit to Monsieur l'Abbé. He would have given me news of you. Perhaps, in about ten days, you will write to my sister — a little note of three or four lines — it will not take much of your time — just to tell her how you are, and that you do not forget us."

"Oh, as to forgetting you, as to losing the remembrance of your extreme kindness, your goodness, never, Miss Percival, never!"

His voice trembled, he was afraid of his own emotion, he rose.

"I assure you, Miss Percival, I must go and speak to your sister. She is looking at me. She must be astonished."

He crossed the room, Bettina followed him with her eyes.

Mrs. Norton had just placed herself at the piano to play a waltz for the young people.

Paul de Lavardens approached Miss Percival.

"Will you do me the honor, Miss Percival?"

"I believe I have just promised this dance to Monsieur Jean," she replied.

"Well, if not to him, will you give it to me?"

"That is understood."

Bettina walked toward Jean, who had seated himself near Mrs. Scott.

"I have just told a dreadful story," said she. "Monsieur de Lavardens has asked me for this dance, and I replied that I had promised it to you. You would like it, wouldn't you?"

To hold her in his arms, to breathe the perfume of her hair — Jean felt his courage could not support this ordeal, he dared not accept.

"I regret extremely I can not, I am not well tonight; I persisted in coming because I would not leave without wishing you good-bye, but dance, no, it is impossible!"

Mrs. Norton began the prelude of the waltz.

"Well," said Paul, coming up quite joyful, "who is it to be, he or I?"

"You," she said, sadly, without removing her eyes from Jean.

She was much disturbed, and replied without knowing well what she said. She immediately regretted having accepted, she would have liked to stay there, near him. But it was too late, Paul took her hand and led her away.

Jean rose; he looked at the two, Bettina and Paul, a haze floated before his eyes, he suffered cruelly.

"There is only one thing I can do," thought he, "profit by this waltz, and go. Tomorrow I will write a few lines to Mrs. Scott to excuse myself."

He gained the door, he looked no more at Bettina; had he looked, he would have stayed.

But Bettina looked at him; and all at once she said to Paul:

"Thank you very much, but I am a little tired, let us stop, please. You will excuse me, will you not?"

Paul offered his arm.

"No, thank you," said she.

The door was just closing, Jean was no longer there. Bettina ran across the room. Paul remained alone, much surprised, understanding nothing of what had passed.

Jean was already at the hall-door, when he heard someone call — "Monsieur Jean! Monsieur Jean!"

He stopped and turned. She was near him.

"You are going without wishing me good-bye?"

"I beg your pardon, I am very tired."

"Then you must not walk home, the weather is threatening," she extended her hand out-of-doors, "it is raining already."

"Come and have a cup of tea in the little drawing room, and I will tell them to drive you home," and turning toward one of the footmen, "tell them to send a carriage round directly."

"No, Miss Percival, pray, the open air will revive me. I must walk, let me go."

"Go, then, but you have no greatcoat, take something to wrap yourself in."

"I shall not be cold — while you with that open dress — I shall go to oblige you to go in." And without even offering his hand, he ran quickly down the steps.

"If I touch her hand," he thought, "I am lost, my secret will escape me."

His secret! He did not know that Bettina read his heart like an open book.

When Jean had descended the steps, he hesitated one short moment, these words were upon his lips:

"I love you, I adore you, and that is why I will see you no more!"

But he did not utter these words, he fled away and was soon lost in the darkness.

Bettina remained there against the brilliant background made by the light from the hall. Great drops of rain, driven by the wind, swept across her bare shoulders and made her shiver; she took no notice, she distinctly heard her heart beat.

"I knew very well that he loved me," she thought, "but now I am very sure, that I, too — oh! yes! I, too! —"

All at once, in one of the great mirrors in the hall door, she saw the reflection of the two footmen who stood there motionless, near the oak table in the hall. Bettina heard bursts of laughter and the strains of the waltz; she stopped. She wished to be alone, completely alone, and addressing one of the servants, she said:

"Go and tell your mistress that I am very tired, and have gone to my own room."

Annie, her maid, had fallen asleep, in an easy chair. She sent her away. She would undress herself. She let herself sink on a couch, she was oppressed with delicious emotion.

The door of her room opened, it was Mrs. Scott.

"You are not well, Bettina?"

"Oh, Susie, is it you, my Susie? how nice of you to come. Sit here, close to me, quite close to me."

She hid herself like a child in the arms of her sister, caressing with her burning brow Susie's fresh shoulders. Then she suddenly burst into sobs, great sobs, which stifled, suffocated her.

"Bettina, my darling, what is the matter?"

"Nothing, nothing! it is nothing, it is joy — joy!"

"Joy?"

"Yes, yes, wait — let me cry a little, it will do me so much good. But do not be frightened, do not be frightened."

Beneath her sister's caress, Bettina grew calm, soothed.

"It is over, I am better now, and I can talk to you. It is about Jean."

"Jean! You call him Jean?"

"Yes, I call him Jean. Have you not noticed for some time that he was dull and looked quite melancholy?"

"Yes, I have."

"When he came, he went and posted himself near you, and stayed there, silent, absorbed to such a degree, that for several days I asked myself — pardon me for speaking to you with such frankness, it is my way, you know — I asked myself if it were not you whom he loved, Susie; you are so charming, it would have been so natural! But no, it was not you, it was I!"

"You?"

"Yes, I. Listen, he scarcely dared to look at me, he avoided me, he fled from me, he was afraid of me, evidently afraid. Now, in justice, am I a person to inspire fear? I am sure I am not!"

"Certainly not!"

"Ah! it was not I of whom he was afraid, it was my money, my horrid money! This money which attracts all the others and tempts them so much, this money terrifies him, drives him desperate, because he is not like the others, because he —"

"My child, take care, perhaps you are mistaken."

"Oh, no, I am not mistaken! Just now, at the door, when he was going away, he said some words to me. These words were nothing. But if you had seen his distress in spite of all his efforts to control it! Susie, dear Susie, by the affection which I bear you, and God knows how great is that affection, this is my conviction, my absolute conviction — if, instead of being Miss Percival, I had been a poor little girl without a penny Jean would then have taken my hand, and have told me that he loved me, and if he had spoken to me thus, do you know what I should have replied?"

"That you loved him, too?"

"Yes; and that is why I am so happy. With me it is a fixed idea that I must adore the man who will be my husband. Well! I don't say that I adore Jean, no, not yet; but still it is beginning, Susie, and it is beginning so sweetly."

"Bettina, it really makes me uneasy to see you in this state of excitement. I do not deny that Monsieur Reynaud is much attached to you —"

"Oh, more than that, more than that!"

"Loves you, if you like; yes, you are right, you are quite right. He loves you; and are you not worthy, my darling, of all the love that one can bear you? As to Jean — it is progressing decidedly, here am I also calling him Jean — well! you know what I think of him. I rank him very, very high. But in spite of that, is he really a suitable husband for you?"

"Yes, if I love him."

"I am trying to talk sensibly to you, and you, on the contrary — Understand me, Bettina; I have an experience of the world which you can not have. Since our arrival in Paris, we have been launched into a very brilliant, very animated, very aristocratic society. You might have been already, if you had liked, marchioness or princess."

"Yes, but I did not like."

"It would not matter to you to be called Madame Reynaud?"

"Not in the least, if I love him."

"Ah! you return always to —"

"Because that is the true question. There is no other. Now I will be sensible in my turn. This question — I grant that this is not quite settled, and that I have, perhaps, allowed myself to be too easily persuaded. You see how sensible I am. Jean is going away tomorrow, I shall not see him again for three weeks. During these three weeks I shall have ample time to question myself, to examine myself, in a word, to know my own mind. Under my giddy manner, I am serious and thoughtful, you know that?"

"Oh, yes, I know it."

"Well, I will make this petition to you, as I would have addressed it to our mother had she been here. If, in three weeks, I say to you, 'Susie, I am certain that I love him,' will you allow me to go to him, myself, quite alone, and ask him if he will have me for his wife? That is what you did with Richard. Tell me, Susie, will you allow me?"

"Yes, I will allow you."

Bettina embraced her sister, and murmured these words in her ear:

"Thank you, mamma."

"Mamma, mamma! It was thus that you used to call me when you were a child, when we were alone in the world together, when I used to undress you in our poor room in New York, when I held you in my arms, when I laid you in your little bed, when I sang you to sleep. And since then, Bettina, I have had only one desire in the world, your happiness. That is why I beg you to reflect well. Do not answer me, do not let us talk anymore of that. I wish to leave you very calm, very tranquil. You have sent away Annie, would you like me to be your little mamma again tonight, to undress you, and put you to bed as I used to do?"

"Yes, I should like it very much."

"And when you are in bed, you promise me to be very good?"

"As good as an angel."

"You will do your best to go to sleep?"

"My very best."

"Very quietly, without thinking of anything?"

"Very quietly, without thinking of anything."

"Very well, then."

Ten minutes after, Bettina's pretty head rested gently amid embroideries and lace. Susie said to her sister:

"I am going down to those people who bore me dreadfully this evening. Before going to my own room, I shall come back and see if you are asleep. Do not speak. Go to sleep."

She went away. Bettina remained alone; she tried to keep her word; she endeavored to go to sleep, but only half-succeeded. She fell into a half-slumber which left her floating between dream and reality. She had promised to think of nothing, and yet she thought of him, always of him, of nothing but him, vaguely, confusedly.

How long a time passed thus she could not tell.

All at once it seemed to her that someone was walking in her room; she half-opened her eyes, and thought she recognized her sister. In a very sleepy voice she said to her:

"You know I love him."

"Hush! go to sleep."

"I am asleep! I am asleep!"

At last she did fall sound asleep, less profoundly, however, than usual, for about four o'clock in the morning she was suddenly awakened by a noise, which, the night before, would not have disturbed her slumber. The rain fell in torrents, and beat against her window.

"Oh, it is raining!" she thought. "He will get wet."

That was her first thought. She rose, crossed the room barefooted, half-opened the shutters. The day had broke, grey and lowering; the clouds were heavy with rain, the wind blew tempestuously, and drove the rain in gusts before it.

Bettina did not go back to bed, she felt it would be quite impossible to sleep again. She put on a dressing gown, and remained at the window; she watched the falling rain. Since he positively must go, she would have liked the weather to be fine; she would have liked bright sunshine to have cheered his first day's march.

When she came to Longueval a month ago, Bettina did not know what this meant. But she knew it now. A day's march for the artillery is twenty or thirty miles, with an hour's halt for luncheon. It was the Abbé Constantin who had taught her that; when going their rounds in the morning among the poor, Bettina overwhelmed the Curé with questions on military affairs, and particularly on the artillery.

Twenty or thirty miles under this pouring rain! Poor Jean! Bettina thought of young Turner, young Norton, of Paul de Lavardens, who would sleep calmly till ten in the morning, while Jean was exposed to this deluge.

Paul de Lavardens!

This name awoke in her a painful memory, the memory of that waltz the evening before. To have danced like that, while Jean was so obviously in trouble! That waltz took the proportions of a crime in her eyes; it was a horrible thing that she had done.

And then, had she not been wanting in courage and frankness in that last interview with Jean? He neither could nor dared say anything; but she might have shown more tenderness, more expansiveness. Sad and suffering as he was, she should never have allowed him to go back on foot. She ought to have detained him at any price. Her imagination tormented and excited her; Jean must have carried away with him the impression that she was a bad little creature, heartless and pitiless. And in half-an-hour he was going away, away for three weeks. Ah! if she could by any means — but there is a way! The regiment must pass along the wall of the park, under the terrace.

Bettina was seized with a wild desire to see Jean pass; he would understand well, if he saw her at such an hour, that she had come to beg his pardon for her cruelty of the previous evening. Yes, she would go! But she had promised to Susie to be as good as an angel, and to do what she was going to do, was that being as good as an angel? She would make up for it by acknowledging all to Susie when she came in again, and Susie would forgive her.

She would go! She had made up her mind. Only how should she dress herself? She had nothing at hand but a muslin dressing gown, little high-heeled slippers, and blue satin shoes. She might wake her maid. Oh, never would she dare to do that, and time pressed; a quarter to five! the regiment would start at five o'clock.

She might, perhaps, manage with the muslin dressing gown, and the satin shoes; in the hall, she might find her hat, her little sabots which she wore in the garden, and the large tartan cloak for driving in wet weather. She half-opened her door with infinite precautions. Everything slept in the house; she crept along the corridor, she descended the staircase.

If only the little sabots are there in their place; that is her great anxiety. There they are! She slips them on over her satin shoes, she wraps herself in her great mantle.

She hears that the rain has redoubled in violence. She notices one of those large umbrellas which the footmen use on the box in wet weather; she seizes it; she is ready; but when she is ready to go, she sees that the hall-door is fastened by a great iron bar. She tries to raise it; but the bolt holds fast, resists all her efforts, and the great clock in the hall slowly strikes five. He is starting at that moment.

She will see him! she will see him! Her will is excited by these obstacles. She makes a great effort; the bar yields, slips back in the groove. But Bettina has made a long scratch on her hand, from which issues a slender stream of blood. Bettina twists her handkerchief round her hand, takes her great umbrella, turns the key in the lock; and opens the door.

At last she is out of the house!

The weather is frightful. The wind and the rain rage together. It takes five or six minutes to reach the terrace which looks over the road. Bettina darts forward courageously; her head bent, hidden under her immense umbrella, she has taken a few steps. All at once, furious, mad, blinding, a sudden squall bursts upon Bettina, buries her in her mantle, drives her along, lifts her almost from the ground, turns the umbrella violently inside out; that is nothing, the disaster is not yet complete.

Bettina has lost one of her little sabots; they were not practical sabots; they were only pretty little things for fine weather, and at this moment, when Bettina struggles against the tempest with her blue satin shoe half buried in the wet gravel, at this moment the wind bears to her the distant echo of a blast of trumpets. It is the regiment starting!

Bettina makes a desperate effort, abandons her umbrella, finds her little sabot, fastens it on as well as she can, and starts off running, with a deluge descending on her head.

At last, she is in the wood, the trees protect her a little. Another blast, nearer this time. Bettina fancies she hears the rolling of the gun-carriages. She makes a last effort, there is the terrace, she is there just in time.

Twenty yards off she perceived the white horses of the trumpeters, and along the road caught glimpses, vaguely appearing through the fog, of the long line of guns and wagons.

She sheltered herself under one of the old limes which bordered the terrace. She watched, she waited. He is there among that confused mass of riders. Will she be able to recognize him? And he, will he see her? Will any chance make him turn his head that way?

Bettina knows that he is Lieutenant in the second battery of his regiment; she knows that a battery is composed of six guns, and six ammunition wagons. Of course it is the Abbé Constantin who has taught her that. Thus she must allow the first battery to pass, that is to say, count six guns, six wagons, and then — he will be there.

There he is at last, wrapped in his great cloak, and it is he who sees, who recognizes her first. A few moments before, he had recalled to his mind a long walk which he had taken with her one evening, when night was falling, on that terrace. He raised his eyes, and the very spot where he remembered having seen her, was the spot where he found her again. He bowed, and, bareheaded in the rain, turning round in his saddle, as long as he could see her, he looked at her. He said again to himself what he had said the previous evening:

"It is for the last time."

With a charming gesture of both hands, she returned his farewell, and this gesture, repeated many times, brought her hands so near, so near her lips, that one might have fancied —

"Ah!" she thought, "if, after that, he does not understand that I love him, and does not forgive me my money!"

Chapter IX

THE REWARD OF TENDER COURAGE

*I*t was the 20th of August, the day which should bring Jean back to Longueval.

Bettina awoke very early, rose, and ran immediately to the window. The evening before, the sky had looked threatening, heavy with clouds. Bettina slept but little, and all night prayed that it might not rain the next day.

In the early morning a dense fog enveloped the park of Longueval, the trees of which were hidden from view, as by a curtain. But gradually the rays of the sun dissipated the mist, the trees became vaguely discernible through the vapor; then, suddenly, the sun shone brilliantly, flooding with light the park, and the fields beyond; and the lake, where the black swans were disporting themselves in the radiant light, appeared as bright as a sheet of polished metal.

The weather was going to be beautiful. Bettina was a little superstitious. The sunshine gives her good hope and good courage. "The day begins well, so it will finish well."

Mr. Scott had come home several days before. Susie, Betting, and the children waited on the quay at Havre for the arrival of his steamer.

They exchanged many tender embraces; then, Richard, addressing his sister-in-law, said, laughingly:

"Well, when is the wedding to be?"

"What wedding?"

"Yours."

"My wedding?"

"Yes, certainly."

"And to whom am I about to be married?"

"To Monsieur Jean Reynaud."

"Ah! Susie has written to you?"

"Susie? Not at all. Susie has not said a word. It is you, Bettina, who have written to me. For the last two months, all your letters have been occupied with this young officer."

"All my letters?"

"Yes, and you have written to me oftener and more at length than usual. I do not complain of that, but I do ask when you are going to present me with a brother-in-law?"

He spoke jestingly, but Bettina replied:

"Soon, I hope."

Mr. Scott perceived that the affair was serious. When returning in the carriage, Bettina asked Mr. Scott if he had kept her letters.

"Certainly," he replied.

She read them again. It was indeed only with "Jean" that all these letters have been filled. She found therein related, down to the most trifling details, their first meeting. There was the portrait of Jean in the vicarage garden, with his straw hat and his earthenware salad-dish — and then it was again Monsieur Jean, always Monsieur Jean. She discovered that she had loved him much longer than she had suspected. At last it was the 10th of August. Luncheon was just over, and Harry and Bella were impatient. They knew that between one and two o'clock the regiment must pass through the village. They had been promised that they should be taken to see the soldiers pass, and for them, as well as for Bettina, the return of the 9th Artillery was a great event.

"Aunt Betty," said Bella, "Aunt Betty, come with us."

"Yes, do come," said Harry, "do come, we shall see our friend Jean, on his big grey horse."

Bettina resisted, refused — and yet how great was the temptation. But no, she would not go, she would not see Jean again till the evening, when she would give him that decisive explanation for which she had been preparing herself for the last three weeks. The children went away with their governesses. Bettina, Susie, and Richard went to sit in the park, quite close to the castle, and as soon as they were established there:

"Susie," said Bettina, "I am going to remind you today of your promise; you remember what passed between us the night of his departure; we settled that if, on the day of his return, I could say to you, 'Susie, I am sure that I love him,' we settled that you would allow me to speak frankly to him, and ask him if he would have me for his wife."

"Yes, I did promise you. But are you very sure?"

"Absolutely — and now the time has come to redeem your promise. I warn you that I intend to bring him to this very place," she added, smiling, "to this seat; and to use almost the same language to him that you formerly used to Richard. You were successful, Susie, you are perfectly happy, and I — that is what I wish to be."

"Richard, Susie has told you about Monsieur Reynaud."

"Yes, and she has told me that there is no man of whom she has a higher opinion, but —"

"But she has told you that for me it would be a rather quiet, rather commonplace marriage. Oh, naughty sister! Will you believe it, Richard, that I can not get this fear out of her head? She does not understand that, before everything, I wish to love and be loved; will you believe it, Richard, that only last week she laid a horrible trap for me? You know that there exists a certain Prince Romanelli."

"Yes, I know you might have been a princess."

"That would not have been immensely difficult, I believe. Well, one day I was so foolish as to say to Susie, that, in extremity, I might accept the Prince Romanelli. Now, just imagine what she did. The Turners were at Trouville, Susie had arranged a little plot. We lunched with the Prince, but the result was disastrous. Accept him! The two hours that I passed with him, I passed in asking myself how I could have said such a thing. No, Richard; no, Susie; I will be neither princess, nor marchioness, nor countess. My wish is to be Madame Jean Reynaud; if, however, Monsieur Jean Reynaud will agree to it, and that is by no means certain."

The regiment entered the village, and suddenly military music burst martial and joyous across the space. All three remained silent, it was the regiment, it was Jean who passed; the sound became fainter, died away, and Bettina continued:

"No, that is not certain. He loves me, however, and much, but without knowing well what I am; I think that I deserve to be loved differently; I think that I should not cause him so much terror, so much fear, if he knew me better, and that is why I ask you to permit me to speak to him this evening freely, from my heart."

"We will allow you," replied Richard, "you shall speak to him freely, for we know, both of us, Bettina, that you will never do anything that is not noble and generous."

"At least, I shall try."

The children ran up to them; they had seen Jean, he was quite white with dust, he said good-morning to them.

"Only," added Bella, "he is not very nice, he did not stop to talk to us; usually he stops, but this time he wouldn't."

"Yes, he would," replied Harry, "for at first he seemed as if he were going to — and then he would not, he went away."

"Well, he didn't stop, and it is so nice to talk to a soldier, especially when he is on horseback."

"It is not that only, it is that we are very fond of Monsieur Jean; if you knew, papa, how kind he is, and how nicely he plays with us."

"And what beautiful drawings he makes. Harry, you remember that great Punch who was so funny, with his stick, you know?"

"And the dog, there was the little dog, too, as in the show."

The two children went away talking of their friend Jean.

"Decidedly," said Mr. Scott, "everyone likes him in this house."

"And you will be like everyone else when you know him," replied Bettina.

The regiment broke into a trot along the highroad, after leaving the village. There was the terrace where Bettina had been the other morning. Jean said to himself:

"Supposing she should be there."

He dreaded and hoped it at the same time. He raised his head, he looked, she was not there.

He had not seen her again, he would not see her again, for a long-time at least. He would start that very evening at six o'clock for Paris; one of the personages in the War Office was interested in him; he would try to get exchanged into another regiment.

Alone at Cercottes, Jean had had time to reflect deeply, and that was the result of his reflections. He could not, he must not, be Bettina Percival's husband.

The men dismounted at the barracks, Jean took leave of his Colonel, his comrades; all was over. He was free, he could go.

But he did not go; he looked around him. How happy he was three months ago, when he rode out of that great yard amid the noise of the cannon rolling over the pavement of Souvigny; but how sadly he should ride away today! Formerly his life was there; where would it be hereafter?

He returned, went to his own room, and wrote to Mrs. Scott; he told her that his duties obliged him to leave immediately, he could not dine at the castle, and begged Mrs. Scott to remember him to Miss Bettina. Bettina, ah! what trouble it cost him to write that name. He closed his letter; he would send it directly.

He made his preparations for departure; then he went to wish his godfather farewell. That is what cost him most; he must speak to him only of a short absence.

He opened one of the drawers of his bureau to take out some money. The first thing that met his eyes was a little note on bluish paper; it was the only note which he had ever received from her.

"Will you have the kindness to give to the servant the book of which you spoke yesterday evening. Perhaps it will be a little serious for me, but yet I should like to try to read it. We shall see you tonight; come as early as possible." It was signed "Bettina."

Jean read and re-read these few lines, but soon he could read them no longer, his eyes were dim.

"It is all that is left me of her," he thought.

At the same moment the Abbé Constantin was tête-à-tête with old Pauline, they were making up their accounts. The financial situation was admirable; more than 2,000 francs in hand! And the wishes of Susie and Bettina were accomplished, there were no more poor in the neighborhood. His old servant, Pauline, had even occasional scruples of conscience.

"You see, Monsieur le Curé," said she, "perhaps we give them a little too much. Then it will be spread about in other parishes that here they can always find charity. And do you know what will happen then, one of these days? Poor people will come and settle in Longueval."

The Curé gave fifty francs to Pauline. She went to take them to a poor man who had broken his arm a few days before, by falling from the top of a hay-cart.

The Abbé Constantin remained alone in the vicarage. He was rather anxious. He had watched for the passing of the regiment; but Jean only stopped for a moment, he looked sad. For some time, the Abbé had noticed that Jean had no longer the flow of good-humor and gayety he once possessed.

The Curé did not disturb himself too much about it, believing it to be one of those little youthful troubles which did not concern a poor old priest. But, on this occasion, Jean's disturbance was very perceptible.

"I will come back directly," he said to the Curé, "I want to speak to you."

He turned abruptly away. The Abbé Constantin had not even had time to give Loulou his piece of sugar, or rather his pieces of sugar, for he had put five or six in his pocket, considering that Loulou had well deserved this feast by ten long days' march, and a score of nights passed under the open sky.

Besides, since Mrs. Scott had lived at Longueval, Loulou had very often had several pieces of sugar; the Abbé Constantin had become extravagant, prodigal; he felt himself a millionaire, the sugar for Loulou was one of his follies. One day, even, he had been on the point of addressing to Loulou his everlasting little speech:

"This comes from the new mistresses of Longueval; pray for them tonight."

It was three o'clock when Jean arrived at the vicarage, and the Curé said, immediately:

"You told me that you wanted to speak to me; what is it about?"

"About something, my dear godfather, which will surprise you, will grieve you —"

"Grieve me!"

"Yes, and which grieves me, too — I have come to bid you farewell."

"Farewell! you are going away?"

"Yes, I am going away."

"When?"

"Today, in two hours."

"In two hours? But, my dear boy, you were going to dine at the castle tonight."

"I have just written to Mrs. Scott to excuse me. I am positively obliged to go."

"Directly?"

"Directly."

"And where are you going?"

"To Paris."

"To Paris! Why this sudden determination?"

"Not so very sudden! I have thought about it for a long time."

"And you have said nothing about it to me! Jean, something has happened. You are a man, and I have no longer the right to treat you as a child; but you know how much I love you; if you have vexations, troubles, why not tell them to me? I could perhaps advise you. Jean, why go to Paris?"

"I did not wish to tell you, it will give you pain; but you have the right to know. I am going to Paris to ask to be exchanged into another regiment."

"Into another regiment! To leave Souvigny!"

"Yes, that is just it; I must leave Souvigny for a short time, for a little while only; but to leave Souvigny is necessary, it is what I wish above all things."

"And what about me, Jean, do you not think of me? A little while! A little while! But that is all that remains to me of life, a little while. And during these last days, that I owe to the grace of God, it was my happiness, yes, Jean, my happiness, to feel you here, near me, and now you are going away! Jean, wait a little patiently, it can not be for very long now for. Wait until the good God has called me to himself, wait till I shall be gone, to meet there, at his side, your father and your mother. Do not go, Jean, do not go."

"If you love me, I love you, too, and you know it well."

"Yes, I know it."

"I have just the same affection for you now that I had when I was quite little, when you took me to yourself, when you brought me up. My heart has not changed, will never change. But if duty — if honor — oblige me to go?"

"Ah, if it is duty, if it is honor, I say nothing more, Jean, that stands before all! — all! — all! I have always known you a good judge of your duty, your honor. Go, my boy, go, I ask you nothing more, I wish to know no more."

"But I wish to tell you all," cried Jean, vanquished by his emotion, "and it is better that you should know all. You will stay here, you will return to the castle, you will see her again — her!"

"See her! Who?"

"Bettina!"

"Bettina?"

"I adore her, I adore her!"

"Oh, my poor boy!"

"Pardon me for speaking to you of these things; but I tell you as I would have told my father."

"And then, I have not been able to speak of it to anyone, and it stifled me; yes, it is a madness which has seized me, which has grown upon me, little by little, against my will, for you know very-well — My God! It was here that I began to love her. You know, when she came here with her sister — with the little *rouleaux* of francs — her hair fell down — and then the evening, the month of Mary! Then I was permitted to see her freely, familiarly, and you, yourself, spoke to me constantly of her. You praised her sweetness, her goodness. How often have you told me that there was no one in the world better than she is!"

"And I thought it, and I think it still. And no one here knows her better than I do, for it is I alone who have seen her with the poor. If you only knew how tender, and how good she is! Neither wretchedness nor suffering repulse her. But, my dear boy, I am wrong to tell you all this."

"No, no, I will see her no more, I promise you; but I like to hear you speak of her."

"In your whole life, Jean, you will never meet a better woman, nor one who has more elevated sentiments. To such a point, that one day — she had taken me with her in an open carriage, full of toys — she was taking these toys to a poor sick little girl, and when she gave them to her, to make the poor little thing laugh, to amuse her, she talked so prettily to her that I thought of you, and I said to myself, I remember it now, 'Ah, if she were poor!'"

"Ah! if she were poor, but she is not."

"Oh, no! But what can you do, my poor child! If it gives you pain to see her, to live near her; above all, if it will prevent you suffering — go, go — and yet, and yet —"

The old priest became thoughtful, let his head fall between his hands, and remained silent for some moments; then he continued:

"And yet, Jean, do you know what I think? I have seen a great deal of Mademoiselle Bettina since she came to Longueval. Well — when I reflect — it did not astonish me that anyone should be interested in you, for it seemed so natural — but she talked always, yes, always of you."

"Of me?"

"Yes, of you, and of your father and mother; she was curious to know how you lived. She begged me to explain to her what a soldier's life was, the life of a true soldier, who loved his profession, and performed his duties conscientiously."

"It is extraordinary, since you have told me this, recollections crowd upon me, a thousand little things collect and group themselves together. They returned from Havre yesterday at three o'clock. Well! an hour after their arrival she was here. And it was of you of whom she spoke directly. She asked if you had written to me, if you had not been ill, when you would arrive, at what hour, if the regiment would pass through the village?"

"It is useless at this moment, my dear godfather," said Jean, "to recall all these memories."

"No, it is not useless. She seemed so pleased, so happy even, that she should see you again! She would make quite a fête of the dinner this evening. She would introduce you to her brother-in-law, who has come back. There is no one else in the house at this moment, not a single visitor. She insisted strongly on this point, and I remember her last words — she was there, on the threshold of the door:

"'There will be only five of us,' she said, 'you and Monsieur Jean, my sister, my brother-in-law, and myself.'

"And then she added, laughing, 'Quite a family party.'

"With these words she went, she almost ran away. Quite a family party! Do you know what I think, Jean? Do you know?"

"You must not think that, you must not."

"Jean, I believe that she loves you."

"And I believe it, too."

"You, too!"

"When I left her, three weeks ago, she was so agitated, so moved! She saw me sad and unhappy, she would not let me go. It was at the door of the castle. I was obliged to tear myself, yes, literally tear myself away. I should have spoken, burst out, told her all. After I had gone a few steps, I stopped and turned. She could no longer see me, I was lost in the darkness; but I could see her. She stood there motionless, her shoulders and arms bare, in the rain, her eyes fixed on the way by which I had gone. Perhaps I am mad to think that. Perhaps it was only a feeling of pity. But no, it was something more than pity, for do you know what she did the next morning? She came at five o'clock, in the most frightful weather, to see me pass with the regiment — and then — the way she bade me adieu — oh, my friend, my dear old friend!"

"But then," said the poor Curé, completely bewildered, completely at a loss, "but then, I do not understand you at all. If you love her, Jean, and if she loves you?"

"But that is, above all, the reason why I must go. If it were only I, if I were certain that she has not perceived my love, certain that she has not been touched by it, I would stay, I would stay — for nothing but for the sweet joy of seeing her, and I would love her from afar, without any hope, for nothing but the happiness of loving her. But no, she has understood too well, and far from discouraging me — that is what forces me to go."

"No, I do not understand it! I know well, my poor boy, we are speaking of things in which I am no great scholar, but you are both good, young, and charming; you love her, she would love you, and you will not!"

"And her money! her money!"

"What matters her money? If it is only that, is it because of her money that you have loved her? It is rather in spite of her money. Your conscience, my son, would be quite at peace with regard to that, and that would suffice."

"No, that would not suffice. To have a good opinion of one's self is not enough; that opinion must be shared by others."

"Oh, Jean! Among all who know you, who can doubt you?"

"Who knows? And then there is another thing besides this question of money, another thing more serious and more grave. I am not the husband suited to her."

"And who could be more worthy than you?"

"The question to be considered is not my worth; we have to consider what she is and what I am, to ask what ought to be her life, and what ought to be my life."

"One day, Paul — you know he has rather a blunt way of saying things, but that very bluntness often places thoughts much more distinctly before us — Paul was speaking of her; he did not suspect anything; if he had, he is good-natured, he would not have spoken thus — well, he said to me:

"'What she needs is a husband who would be entirely devoted to her, to her alone, a husband who would have no other care than to make her existence a perpetual holiday, a husband who would give himself, his whole life, in return for her money.'

"You know me; such a husband I can not, I must not be. I am a soldier, and shall remain one. If the chances of my career sent me some day to a garrison in the depths of the Alps, or in some almost unknown village in Algeria, could I ask her to follow me? Could I condemn her to the life of a soldier's wife, which is in some degree the life of a soldier himself? Think of the life which she leads now, of all that luxury, of all those pleasures!"

"Yes," said the Abbé, "that is more serious than the question of money."

"So serious that there is no hesitation possible. During the three weeks that I passed alone in the camp, I have well considered all that; I have thought of nothing else, and loving her as I do love, the reason must indeed be strong which shows me clearly my duty. I must go, I must go far, very far away, as far as possible. I shall suffer much, but I must not see her again! I must not see her again!"

Jean sank on a chair near the fireplace. He remained there quite overpowered with his emotion. The old priest looked at him.

"To see you suffer, my poor boy! That such suffering should fall upon you! It is too cruel, too unjust!"

At that moment someone knocked gently at the door.

"Ah!" said the Curé, "do not be afraid, Jean. I will send them away."

The Abbé went to the door, opened it, and recoiled as if before an unexpected apparition.

It was Bettina. In a moment she had seen Jean, and going direct to him:

"You!" cried she. "Oh, how glad I am!"

He rose. She took his hands, and addressing the Curé, she said:

"I beg your pardon, Monsieur le Curé, for going to him first. You, I saw yesterday, and him, not for three whole weeks, not since a certain night, when he left our house, sad and suffering."

She still held Jean's hands. He had neither power to make a movement nor to utter a sound.

"And now," continued Betting, "are you better? No, not yet; I can see, still sad. Ah, I have done well to come! It was an inspiration! However, it embarrasses me a little, it embarrasses me a great deal, to find you here. You will understand why when you know what I have come to ask of your godfather."

She relinquished his hands, and turning toward the Abbé, said:

"I have come to beg you to listen to my confession — yes, my confession. But do not go away, Monsieur Jean; I will make my confession publicly. I am quite willing to speak before you, and now I think of it, it will be better thus. Let us sit down, shall we?"

She felt herself full of confidence and daring. She burned with fever, but with that fever which, on the field of battle, gives to a soldier ardor, heroism, and disdain of danger. The emotion which made Bettina's heart beat quicker than usual was a high and generous emotion. She said to herself:

"I will be loved! I will love! I will be happy! I will make him happy! And since he has not sufficient courage to do it, I must have it for both. I must march alone, my head high, and my heart at ease, to the conquest of our love, to the conquest of our happiness!"

From her first words Bettina had gained over the Abbé and Jean a complete ascendancy. They let her say what she liked, they let her do as she liked, they felt that the hour was supreme; they understood that what was happening would be decisive, irrevocable, but neither was in a position to foresee.

They sat down obediently, almost automatically; they waited, they listened. Alone, of the three, Bettina retained her composure. It was in a calm and even voice that she began.

"I must tell you first, Monsieur le Curé, to set your conscience quite at rest, I must tell you that I am here with the consent of my sister and my brother-in-law. They know why I have come; they know what I am about to do. They not only know, but they approve. That is settled, is it not? Well, what brings me here is your letter, Monsieur Jean, that letter in which you tell my sister that you can not dine with us this evening, and that you are positively obliged to leave here. This letter has unsettled all my plans. I had intended, this evening — of course with the permission of my sister and brother-in-law — I had intended, after dinner, to take you into the park, to seat myself with you on a bench; I was childish enough to choose the place beforehand."

"There I should have delivered a little speech, well prepared, well studied, almost learned by heart, for since your departure I have scarcely thought of anything else; I repeat it to myself from morning to night. That is what I had proposed to do, and you understand that your letter caused me much embarrassment. I reflected a little, and thought that if I addressed my little speech to your godfather it would be almost the same as if I addressed it to you. So I have come, Monsieur le Curé, to beg you to listen to me."

"I will listen to you, Miss Percival," stammered the Abbé.

"I am rich, Monsieur le Curé, I am very rich, and to speak frankly I love my wealth very much-yes, very much. To it I owe the luxury which surrounds me, luxury which, I acknowledge — it is a confession — is by no means disagreeable to me. My excuse is that I am still very young; it will perhaps pass as I grow older, but of that I am not very sure. I have another excuse; it is, that if I love money a little for the pleasure that it procures me, I love it still more for the good which it allows me to do. I love it — selfishly, if you like — for the joy of giving, but I think that my fortune is not very badly placed in my hands. Well, Monsieur le Curé, in the same way that you have the care of souls, it seems that I have the care of money. I have always thought, 'I wish, above all things, that my husband should be worthy of sharing this great fortune. I wish to be very sure that he will make a good use of it with me while I am here, and after me, if I must leave this world first.' I thought of another thing; I thought, 'He who will be my husband must be someone I can love!' And now, Monsieur le Curé, this is where my confession really begins. There is a man, who for the last two months, has done all he can to conceal from me that he loves me; but I do not doubt that this man loves me. You do love me, Jean?"

"Yes," said Jean, in a low voice, his eyes cast down, looking like a criminal, "I do love you!"

"I knew it very well, but I wanted to hear you say it, and now I entreat you, do not utter a single word. Any words of yours would be useless, would disturb me, would prevent me from going straight to my aim, and telling you what I positively intend to say. Promise me to stay there, sitting still, without moving, without speaking. You promise me?"

"I promise you."

Bettina, as she went on speaking, began to lose a little of her confidence, her voice trembled slightly. She continued, however, with a gayety that was a little forced:

"Monsieur le Curé, I do not blame you for what has happened, yet all this is a little your fault."

"My fault!"

"Ah! do not speak, not even you. Yes, I repeat it, your fault. I am certain that you have spoken well of me to Jean, much too well. Perhaps, without that, he would not have thought — And at the same time you have spoken very well of him to me. Not too well — no, no — but yet very well! Then, I had so much confidence in you, that I began to look at him, and examine, him with a little more attention. I began to compare him with those who, during the last year, had asked my hand. It seemed to me that he was in every respect superior to them.

"At last, it happened, on a certain day, or rather on a certain evening-three weeks ago, the evening before you left here, Jean — I discovered that I loved you. Yes, Jean, I love you! I entreat you, do not speak; stay where you are; do not come near me.

"Before I came here, I thought I had supplied myself with a good stock of courage, but you see I have no longer my fine composure of a minute ago. But I have still something to tell you, and the most important of all. Jean, listen to me well; I do not wish for a reply torn from your emotion; I know that you love me. If you marry me, I do not wish it to be only for love; I wish it to be also for reason. During the fortnight before you left here, you took so much pains to avoid me, to escape any conversation, that I have not been able to show myself to you as I am. Perhaps there are in me certain qualities which you do not suspect.

"Jean, I know what you are, I know to what I should bind myself in marrying you, and I should be for you not only the loving and tender woman, but the courageous and constant wife. I know your entire life; your godfather has related it to me. I know why you became a soldier; I know what duties, what sacrifices, the future may demand from you. Jean, do not suppose that I shall turn you from any of these duties, from any of these sacrifices. If I could be disappointed with you for anything, it would be, perhaps, for this thought — oh, you must have had it! — that I should wish you free, and quite my own, that I should ask you to abandon your career. Never! never! Understand well, I shall never ask such a thing of you.

"A young girl whom I know did that when she married, and she did wrong. I love you, and I wish you to be just what you are. It is because you live differently from, and better than, those who have before desired me for a wife, that I desire you for a husband. I should love you less — perhaps I should not love you at all, though that would be very difficult — if you were to begin to live as all those live whom I would not have. When I can follow you, I will follow you; wherever you are will be my duty, wherever you are will be my happiness. And if the day comes when you can not take me, the day when you must go alone, well! Jean, on that day, I promise you to be brave, and not take your courage from you.

"And now, Monsieur le Curé, it is not to him, it is to you that I am speaking; I want you to answer me, not him. Tell me, if he loves me, and feels me worthy of his love, would it be just to make me expiate so severely the fortune that I possess? Tell me, should he not agree to be my husband?"

"Jean," said the old priest, gravely, "marry her. It is your duty, and it will be your happiness!"

Jean approached Bettina, took her in his arms, and pressed upon her brow the first kiss.

Bettina gently freed herself, and addressing the Abbé, said:

"And now, Monsieur l'Abbé, I have still one thing to ask you. I wish — I wish —"

"You wish?"

"Pray, Monsieur le Curé, embrace me, too."

The old priest kissed her paternally on both cheeks, and then Bettina continued:

"You have often told me, Monsieur le Curé, that Jean was almost like your own son, and I shall be almost like your own daughter, shall I not? So you will have two children, that is all."

A month after, on the 12th of September, at mid-day, Bettina, in the simplest of wedding-gowns, entered the church of Longueval, while, placed behind the altar, the trumpets of the 9th Artillery rang joyously through the arches of the old church.

Nancy Turner had begged for the honor of playing the organ on this solemn occasion, for the poor little harmonium had disappeared; an organ, with resplendent pipes, rose in the gallery of the church — it was Miss Percival's wedding present to the Abbé Constantin.

The old Curé said mass, Jean and Bettina knelt before him, he pronounced the benediction, and then remained for some moments in prayer, his arms extended, calling down, with his whole soul, the blessings of Heaven on his two children.

Then floated from the organ the same reverie of Chopin's which Bettina had played the first time that she had entered that little village church, where was to be consecrated the happiness of her life.

And this time it was Bettina who wept.

www.ingramcontent.com/pod-product-compliance
Lightning Source LLC
Chambersburg PA
CBHW030147200626
46812CB00015B/1738